"I can't remember."

It almost broke Nick to see her holding herself as though she was the only person she'd ever been able to depend on. It was enough to propel him forward and hold her.

She was shaking. Maybe they both were, and he boosted her up onto the waist-high counter and let her cling. Let himself soothe.

Three days ago, Dr. Genie Watson had been nothing more than a woman whose reputation for utter brilliance and cool standoffishness was hard to deny.

Now, in just seventy-two short hours, Genie Watson had become so much more to Nick. And he couldn't seem to stop himself from touching her. Wanting her.

He couldn't, shouldn't, *wouldn't* take advantage of her. She was scared, vulnerable. And he was her protector.

"Nick," she whispered, breaking in to his thoughts, "I know that this will be over soon, that they'll find this guy and things will go back to the way they were before. So will you do me a favor and kiss me? Just once, so I know what it's like?"

"Genie, I—" Shouldn't. Couldn't. Wouldn't.

Will.

Dear Harlequin Intrigue Reader,

Beginning this October, Harlequin Intrigue has expanded its lineup to six books! Publishing two more titles each month enables us to bring you an extraordinary selection of breathtaking stories of romantic suspense filled with exciting editorial variety—and we encourage you to try all that we have to offer.

Stock up on catnip! Caroline Burnes brings back your favorite feline sleuth to beckon you into a new mystery in the popular series FEAR FAMILIAR. This four-legged detective sticks his whiskers into the mix to help clear a stunning stuntwoman's name in *Familiar Double*. Up next is Dani Sinclair's new HEARTSKEEP trilogy starting with *The Firstborn*—a darkly sensual gothic romance that revolves around a sinister suspense plot. To lighten things up, bestselling Harlequin American Romance author Judy Christenberry crosses her beloved BRIDES FOR BROTHERS series into Harlequin Intrigue with *Randall Renegade*—a riveting reunion romance that will keep you on the edge of your seat.

Keeping Baby Safe by Debra Webb could either passionately reunite a duty-bound COLBY AGENCY operative and his onetime lover—or tear them apart forever. Don't miss the continuation of this action-packed series. Then Amy J. Fetzer launches our BACHELORS AT LARGE promotion featuring fearless men in blue with *Under His Protection*. Finally, watch for *Dr. Bodyguard* by debut author Jessica Andersen. Will a hunky doctor help penetrate the emotional walls around a lady genius before a madman closes in?

Pick up all six for a complete reading experience you won't forget!

Enjoy,

Denise O'Sullivan
Senior Editor
Harlequin Intrigue

DR. BODYGUARD
JESSICA ANDERSEN

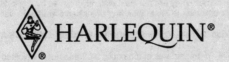

HARLEQUIN®

TORONTO • NEW YORK • LONDON
AMSTERDAM • PARIS • SYDNEY • HAMBURG
STOCKHOLM • ATHENS • TOKYO • MILAN • MADRID
PRAGUE • WARSAW • BUDAPEST • AUCKLAND

ISBN 0-373-22734-5

DR. BODYGUARD

Copyright © 2003 by Dr. Jessica S. Andersen

This edition published by arrangement with Harlequin Books S.A.

® and TM are trademarks of the publisher. Trademarks indicated with ® are registered in the United States Patent and Trademark Office, the Canadian Trade Marks Office and in other countries.

Visit us at www.eHarlequin.com

Printed in U.S.A.

ABOUT THE AUTHOR

Though she's tried out professions ranging from cleaning sea lion cages to cloning glaucoma genes, from patent law to training horses, Jessica is happiest when she's combining all these interests with her first love—writing. These days she's delighted to be writing full-time on a farm in rural Connecticut that she shares will a small menagerie of animals and a hero named Brian. She loves to hear from readers. You can write to her at P.O. Box 204, Voluntown, CT 06384.

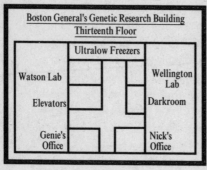

Boston, MASSACHUSETTS

To Nick's Mansion
Theater District
To Genie's Condo

Kneeland Street

To Boston Harbor

Chinatown

Boston General Hospital

Genie's Parking Lot

Boston General's Genetic
Research Building

All underlined places are fictitious.

**Boston General's Genetic Research Building
Thirteenth Floor**

Ultralow Freezers

Watson Lab

Wellington Lab

Elevators

Darkroom

Genie's Office

Nick's Office

CAST OF CHARACTERS

Genie Watson—When the brilliant scientist is brutally attacked and several "accidents" occur in her DNA lab, Genie must turn to co-worker Nick Wellington for protection, even though he's just the type of man she has vowed to avoid.

Nick Wellington—Caught between an ingrained need to protect and a learned distrust of smart, opinionated women who hog lab equipment, Nick fights to save Genie even as he struggles against his growing desires.

George Dixon—He and Genie had once shared a relationship. Now they share a restraining order. How far will he go to get her back?

Richard Fenton Sr.—The aging tycoon is putting financial pressure on Genie to disclose confidential genetic information. Could he be putting another kind of pressure on her, as well?

Richard Fenton Jr.—Heir apparent to his father's fortune, he will do anything to insure his future.

Stephanie Alberts—Genie's clinical coordinator has had terrible luck with men, but she thinks she's found a keeper this time. Or is he just using her?

Roger Strait—Is the salesman from Petrie Pharmaceuticals really Steph's dream come true?

Leo Gabney—One of the top administrators at Boston General Hospital, Leo will do anything to keep the hospital on track. Anything.

For Brian,
who only winced a little
when I announced I was quitting the lab
to write romance novels.

Chapter One

"Wellington? Darn it, Wellington, are you in here?"

Genie shoved at the revolving door and squinted into the research lab's darkroom, trying to pick out her irritating co-worker's broad-shouldered silhouette. She stepped inside, fumbled for a switch and heard the ultrasonic whine of warming red lights over the rumble of machinery. "Because if you're hogging the developer again when my name is clearly written on the sign-up sheet, I'll—"

A blur of motion swept across the faintly red darkness. "Dr. Watson?"

"Wellington, I—" But it hadn't been her floormate's voice. "Who—"

The stranger's hand clamped over her mouth. His hard, hot arm latched on to her ribs and crushed her back against his body. She opened her mouth to scream and tasted the powdered latex of a lab glove. Only a muffled whimper emerged.

"Shut up." His voice was uneven, his breath sour and his silhouette black against the bloody red lights. "Just shut up, slut-doctor-whore. Ruin a man's life and think nothing of it, will you?"

Genie screamed against the glove, thrashed and tried to elbow her captor in the ribs. He cursed and shoved her against the waist-high counter that circled the room. A starburst of pain sang as her hip smacked against something square and solid and red-black.

His heartbeat pounded against her shoulder, quick and scared—or was that hers?—and he thrust against her backside and growled over the clanking hum of the X-ray developer. She tried to wrench away and he pressed harder, pushing her against the counter as she flailed her hands against the warm, red-black air.

She was trapped. Powerless. And her office, safe and bright, wasn't twenty feet away.

"Thought you were safe in your ivory tower, didn't you?" The whisper slid across her skin as his hand cruised up to cup her breast and pinch her nipple through the starched lab coat. "Thought you could take her away from me and I'd do nothing?"

Genie felt her soft leather shoes slide on the linoleum floor as the sharp scent of spilled developer chemicals and madness stung her nose and tears burned her eyes. Shaking her head, she tried to say, *No, no! Why are you doing this? I help people. I don't take them away!* But her struggles only excited him more and he tightened his grip.

"We're smarter than you think, Doctor. We figured out what you and the old man are up to. And we're going to stop you. Permanently. But first..."

He shifted his grip, his intent clear. Oh, God! Genie squealed and kicked backward but encountered only air. Her attacker chuckled and ground her harder against the sink. She whipped her body from side to side in an effort to loosen his hot, trembling arms while her hands groped wildly for a weapon. Something. Anything.

Her grasping fingers glanced off a pair of bandage scissors and sent them spinning to the floor.

Oh, God!

She flailed, straining against his superior strength and trying for the freedom she knew was only a few feet away. Then at the last possible moment, when she heard the rasp of his zipper and felt his cruel, groping hand on her body, Genie touched something else with a straining fingertip.

Something heavy.

Something cold and metal and sharp-cornered.

As his hot fingers slithered up her leg beneath the sensible gray wool skirt, Genie screamed against the impersonal latex glove, grabbed the metal thing and swung it over her shoulder with all her might.

There was a sickening thud as it connected. A bitter curse. Warm wetness sprayed her cheek and the hand fell away from her mouth. She was free!

Then she saw a quick movement of black shadow against the unholy red light.

Pain exploded in her head.

And she saw no more.

"DR. WATSON? Dr. Watson?"

At first the voice reminded her of the loudspeaker at St. Agnes, where she'd done her residency. *Dr. Watson. Paging Dr. Watson. Dr. Watson to the NICU.*

She'd hated the Neonatal Intensive Care Unit, full of sick babies, some born with genetic disorders. For many of the tiny lives in the NICU the cures were few, the costs high, and the bright spark of consciousness too quickly snuffed. Like Marilynn. Poor, dear Marilynn. Genie shuddered and tried to slide deeper into the beckoning blackness.

But the voice wouldn't allow that. "Dr. Watson? Genie? Come on now, wake up."

She must be dreaming. She heard the *rubba-thump, rubba-thump* of the light-proof revolving door and wondered what the light lock was doing in her bedroom.

"Genie? Can you hear me?" For that matter, what was a man's voice doing in her bedroom? The last time that had happened the voice had belonged to the cable guy, and he'd been whiny and had a hanging butt crack the size of a Smithfield ham.

"She's unconscious. And look at all that blood." Another voice murmured agreement as the first one said, "Where the hell are the paramedics? The genetic research building is part of Boston General, for chrissake. The E.R.'s right down the street. What's taking them so long?"

Frustration edged the tone, but the voice was still nice-gruff and interesting, without the nasal twang of Boston. His voice made Genie feel warm and fuzzy and she wanted to snuggle into the sound and bring it with her to the safe darkness.

"Genie? Can you hear me? Open your eyes, sweetheart."

Sweetheart? She liked that. She hadn't been anyone's sweetheart in a long, long time. Not since her father died.

Her eyes remained stubbornly closed when she ordered them to open, but her head began to hurt like hell as if the act had alerted thousands of anxious neurons that she was conscious and ready for pain.

Rubba-thump, rubba-thump. The sound of the revolving light lock magnified the throbbing behind her eyes and she began to feel the hard, cool floor beneath her. This wasn't her bedroom and, oh, she was beginning to hurt.

A new voice, excited. "The police and the paramedics are here." An audible gulp. "Is Dr. Watson going to be okay? That's an awful lot of blood."

"I don't think it's all hers. I hope to hell it's not." She could feel her anchor move away. With a monumental effort she cracked open her eyes and made out a blurry man-shape against the bright, stabbing light.

"Don't leave me. Please." Was that pitiful croak really her own voice? It must have been, because she heard him crouch down beside her, felt him take her hand—

And she slid back into the warm, blessed darkness, taking his presence with her. Feeling safe.

"WHAT THE HELL HAPPENED, Nick?" Leo Gabney looked as though he wanted to yank at his hair as he paced the moss green waiting room at Boston General's E.R. Instead he pulled a soggy handkerchief from his back pocket, wiped it across the top of his glistening scalp, turned and marched back the way he had come.

Nick watched his boss pace and didn't say a word. He'd screwed up, that's what happened. The developer room was across the hall from his office, for God's sake. He should've known something was wrong. He should've been quicker, smarter. *Better,* said the Senator's voice in the back of his head, and Nick twisted his lips in rare agreement.

He'd been annoyed when Jill had told him she hadn't developed yesterday's DNA sequencing because the darkroom was still being used. He'd said something pithy and rude about the one-step-holier-and-a-heck-of-a-lot-smarter-than-the-creator M.D., Ph.D. he was forced to share lab space with and had ignored the Occupied—Please Do Not Enter sign on the darkroom door. He'd simply barged in, intent on giving Dr. Genius a piece of his mind.

The red lights had been on. He'd expected that, since only an idiot would handle autorad film in white light and Dr. Genius was anything but an idiot. But he hadn't expected the little room to be torn apart, with film cassettes opened and scattered willy-nilly and the developer's guts strewn about like spaghetti.

Then he'd stepped further into the room and his foot had slipped on something dark. Something trailing. A black ribbon that led directly to the crumpled lab coat under the sink. He'd flicked on the fluorescents and the red of the dark lights had become a patchwork of macabre crimson splashes on the floor and walls.

Blood. Lots of it. And the motionless body of his archnemesis, Dr. Eugenie Watson, M.D., Ph.D.

"Gentlemen?" The strange voice echoed in the E.R. waiting room and Nick shot to his feet. It wasn't the cops this time. It was a doctor in bloodstained greens.

It was too soon. They couldn't possibly have stopped all that bleeding in so little time. She must've died.

Genius Watson was dead.

Nick remembered that he'd been rude to her that morning in the elevator, more out of habit than any real rancor, and perhaps also because for one brief moment he'd thought she looked nice in the soft gray wool skirt and high-buttoned blouse. Pretty. Touchable.

When a man started thinking of gray wool and lace collars as sexy, he needed to get laid. Fast. Or so he'd thought at the time. Now all he could think was that he'd do anything to go back in time and murder the guy in the darkroom for trashing their experiments and injuring Dr. Watson.

Killing her?

He had a sudden, sharp image of Watson's bloody hand lying in his as they rode to the hospital in the shrieking ambulance. She had begged him not to leave when she should have been cursing him for not finding her sooner. How had he not known something was wrong? He'd been sitting in his office wrestling with that damned journal article. How had he not sensed something? Heard something?

"Is she—" Even Leo Gabney, the most insensitive man Nick had ever met, was unable to finish the question.

"Eugenie Watson is one tough lady."

Nick glanced quickly at the doctor. "Then she's—"

"Going to be fine." Apparently the doctor was familiar with this fill-in-the-blanks form of conversation. "She has a whopping headache and a few stitches to close up the laceration across her eyebrow, but there's no indication of more serious damage.''

"But what about—"

"The blood?" The doctor grinned. "Very little of it was hers. Her attacker must've been a mess when she was through with him. I've discussed it with Detective Sturgeon and he'll put area hospitals on the lookout."

Nick thought about the panty hose torn half off her body. He hated to ask. "Was she—"

The doctor shook his green-capped head. "No evidence of further sexual assault. I'd say she changed his mind by fighting back." Both Nick and Gabney relaxed marginally. The doc continued, "But we can't be sure exactly what happened. She doesn't remember anything about the attack, which isn't surprising if you consider what a horrible experience it must have been. The brain has its own way of protecting itself."

"She doesn't remember anything?" Nick spun toward the new voice, having not realized that Detectives Sturgeon and Peters had entered the room. Sturgeon was sucking one of the peppermints he'd been working his way through ever since he'd arrived at the lab on the heels of the paramedics. His sallow cheeks, moving in and out with each peppermint suck, made him as if he should be behind glass at the Boston Aquarium rather than at the helm of a major investigation. "Is she conscious?"

The doctor wasn't intimidated by Sturgeon's scowl. "She doesn't remember the attack, and she's conscious now but not in any shape to answer questions. You'll have to wait."

Then, just as Nick was coming to like the doctor,

the guy said, "You can make do with this gentleman. He found Miss Watson."

The cops turned with identical fishy looks and Peters flipped to a new page on his pad. "And your name would be?"

Nick sighed. "Dr. Nicholas Wellington the Third, Ph.D."

Sturgeon raised an eyebrow. "Any relation to the Nicholas Wellington that ran for president a few years ago?"

Feeling that helpless mix of guilt and anger that always came with thoughts of the Senator, Nick nodded. "He's my father."

"I'M FINE." Genie batted at the nurse's hands and shooed the blood-pressure cuff away. "I'm a doctor, I should know when I'm okay to leave, don't you think?" The nurse rolled her eyes and glanced at a nearby man in green scrubs as if to say *Not frickin' likely.* The frazzled intern who grinned in reply didn't look a day over fourteen.

Genie winced at the unkind thought. She hadn't been much older than that when she interned—a fact her colleagues never let her live down. She was the last person who should be complaining about her doctor's age, particularly when he was agreeing with her.

"That's correct, you're perfectly fine. Now." He paused for emphasis. "But you know as well as I do that after a concussion of such severity you should be monitored for at least the next twenty-four hours in case there is additional swelling of the brain."

She hated how he said "the brain" as if it belonged to someone else. It was *her* brain damn it, and it had no right to swell without her permission. Since she hadn't given it permission to get any bigger than it already was, she should be able to go home.

But the fourteen-year-old intern remained firm. He crossed his arms over his weedy chest and frowned. "The only way I'm going to release you is if there's somebody with medical training to observe you. Do you have any colleagues you could call? Any friends that could help you?"

Genie opened her mouth to reply, but nothing came out. How pitiful it sounded to say, "No. There's no one." But it was true.

Sure, she had acquaintances. She chatted with the elderly Chinese lady who cleaned the lab each night and she knew the names of all the grandchildren in the pictures that lined Ben's desk at the security kiosk. And she had colleagues that she nodded to in the halls and smiled at in the lunchroom.

But there was nobody to call and say, "I've got a concussion. Will you come stay with me so I can sleep?"

Nobody.

Inexplicably, a low, intimate voice floated through Genie's mind. She didn't clearly remember anything after hearing the *rubba-thump* of the darkroom door behind her when she'd gone to develop the day's films, but she did have a sketchy recollection of a comforting presence in the ambulance. She remembered a large, warm hand holding hers and a gentle voice saying she was going to be okay.

She assumed it had been a paramedic, and made a mental note to thank him for his excellent bedside manner—though with the way her bruised brain was

working, it could be a few weeks before that particular note surfaced.

The nurse and the young intern left in a swirl of
white and green, and when the door swung the other
way, it revealed the face of Genie's least favorite administrator.

She tried to summon a convincing scowl, one that
would soothe the worried look on his face. "Jeez,
Leo, don't I rate anyone better? Couldn't they have
sent Hetta from personnel or Louie from accounts
payable? Even one of Dixon's goons. Anyone would
be a better deathbed visit than you." Though she
didn't like him much as an administrator, Leo was
one of her favorite acquaintances and he smiled at her
feeble snarl.

"Nope, everyone else already had plans. Since neither you nor I have a life, we were unanimously chosen for the roles of visitor and visited." He tried to
grin, but it faltered and his hand trembled as he wiped
a handkerchief across his sweating head. "Jesus, Genie. I... I..." He couldn't finish, just shrugged, and
she wondered if he had been the one to find her in
the darkroom.

She'd seen the bloodstained lab coat before the police had taken it away, but when she tried to imagine
the attack, her mind slid away and showed her other
things instead. Fields. Butterflies. Flowers. The hazy
shape of a man holding his hand out to her.

Since Genie's greatest source of pride was her
well-ordered, methodical mind, she did not like this
open rebellion and planned to make her brain behave
at the earliest possible moment. But to do that, she
had to go home. She'd never get any peace at Boston

General. There would be candy stripers trying to cheer her up until she wanted to throttle them, doctors shining lights in her eyes every five minutes to make sure she wasn't in a coma, and that big woman nurse with the mustache and the sponge baths…

She had to get out of here.

"Will you take me home, Leo?" It was worth a try, but even before the words were out, he shook his head.

"No. No. I don't think that's a good idea, Genie. You're pretty banged up." He paused and she could read the words, *Although it could've been a whole lot worse,* in his gaze. "No. I think you should stay right here and let the doctors look after you while the police find whoever did this."

Genie didn't want to think about who had attacked her. Even the word police made nausea swirl higher and sweat bead. She didn't want to think about being attacked. Not here, not now. She needed to go home.

Needed to be alone so she could fall apart in private.

She frowned to keep the tears away, but the movement pulled at the stitches on her forehead and made her headache worse. "Then go away. I don't want any visitors unless they're going to take me home." She stopped Leo on his way out. "Hey. Can you find the guy that rode with me in the ambulance? I want to thank him."

Leo looked surprised. "You do? But I thought you didn't…" He trailed off, then shrugged. "Okay, I'll go get him."

"He's here?" Didn't paramedics hang out at firehouses? Or in ambulances? She thought so, though her E.R. experience was limited to a quick three-week rotation and taped reruns of the popular television show.

"Yeah, right outside. He's been waiting around to make sure you were going to be okay. He was real worried about you."

"Then send him in and go away, Leo." The administrator headed for the door and Genie called after him, "And, Leo? Thanks for coming. Thanks for looking upset." Even though he was probably more concerned about lawsuits and PR nightmares, it was nice to think that someone cared.

When he was gone, the nausea subsided and was replaced with a warm, fuzzy feeling Genie thought might be due to the little pill Nurse Walrus had given her a few minutes earlier. Her mind drifted.

She needed, she thought irrelevantly, to get a life. If nothing else, this…incident had brought home the fact that she'd let important things slide while she'd pursued her medical degree, then her Ph.D., becoming the youngest Primary Investigator that Boston General had ever seen.

She made another mental note. *Make a few friends. Go on a date.* Her lips curved. A date? With whom? The pool of eligible men at Boston General was pretty shallow. She certainly wasn't dating George Dixon again—been there, done that, got the restraining order—and most of the other researchers she knew were either ancient, married or—as in the case of the handsome antichrist she shared lab space with—egocentric jerks.

At the thought of her worthy opponent, something niggled at the back of Genie's brain, but the rumble of Leo's voice in the hall diverted her and she thought that her paramedic must be pretty inefficient if he waited for each of his patients to wake up. Or else he'd picked up on the same weird vibrations she'd felt run up her arm when he'd been holding her hand in the ambulance.

She plucked at the overwashed sheet and wished she were wearing something other than a hospital johnny. Wished she had a comb and a mirror. Wished she hadn't run out of laundry and been forced to scrounge in the back of her underwear drawer. Her heart sank at the thought of her colleagues at Boston General seeing the zebra striped satin panties and matching bra her mother had optimistically sent from Paris.

Never mind what the paramedic thought, she could just imagine the talk in the doctors' lounge. *Hey, did you see what Watson was wearing when they brought her in? Whoo-whee. Hot stuff for such a cold fish.*

Genie didn't want to be hot stuff. She didn't want to be a cold fish. She just wanted to be—

The door opened. She glanced over to thank her paramedic and perhaps, since there was no time such as the present to work on her new resolve, ask him if she could buy him a drink. But instead her heart gave an unsteady thump and all that came out of her mouth was a startled, "Beef!"

The big blond man at the door stopped, looked intently at her, and a slow, sexy grin creased his face. He nodded and said in a disturbingly familiar drawl—one that could even be called nice if she stretched it—"Genius."

And the battle lines were drawn. Again.

He knew she hated the nickname that had plagued her since she'd skipped fourth and fifth grades, landing smack in junior high at the age of eight. He called her that to bug her, the same reason she called him Beef to his face when the other women did it behind his back.

Nicholas "Beef" Wellington the Third. He might think the nickname was a culinary reference, but the women knew better. They called him Beef as a tribute to his masculine physique, a testimony to his hunkiness and grade-A buns.

Except for Genie. She called him Beef because she knew it irked him and because he was everything she was not—gorgeous, popular, wealthy and well-connected. And sexy. Had she mentioned sexy? He was also sloppy and easygoing, and for the past several months, Leo had forced her to share her precious lab space with him. Her equipment.

Practically her life.

Dr. Genius Watson and Dr. Beef Wellington. They were opposites. Thesis and antithesis. Matter and antimatter. Genie figured that over time they'd either cancel each other out or repel each other into different universes.

She was betting on the latter.

"I was expecting somebody else," she said. "A paramedic." Please, she thought, let it have been a paramedic.

Beef Wellington crossed the room in two ambling strides. His lab coat was unbuttoned and the weight of the ID badge, radiation monitor and pen collection in his left breast pocket pulled the coat askew to give her a quick glimpse of the tight, perfect chest and flat stomach beneath the worn T-shirt. There were rusty stains on his sleeves and on the faded jeans that showed through the gap in the white coat.

His dark blond hair had outgrown its midsummer buzz cut and drooped across his forehead and ears as though it couldn't bear to be away from his face with its wide Viking cheekbones and slashing blade of a nose.

He leaned close and Genie could smell him, a combination of warm soap, acrylamide gel and male musk. He practically oozed pheromones. "Why do you need a paramedic? You sick or something?"

He seemed to have conveniently forgotten that she was lying in a hospital bed with stitches and a concussion. From the way her heart was tap dancing in her chest, she wouldn't doubt a touch of arrhythmia, too.

She started to frown, then winced instead. "Never mind. Why are you here? Wasn't it bad enough the administration inflicted Leo on me? They had to send you, too? Why? So you could gloat about having my equipment to yourself for the rest of the day? I think I'm feeling sicker by the minute."

"Leo said you wanted to see me." Wellington's icy-blue eyes flashed as he said the name. Genie wondered fleetingly what the administrator had done to earn his ire this time—besides making him share lab space with a woman he couldn't stand, of course.

As her hope that she hadn't actually held Wellington's hand started to crumble, Genie tried one last time. "Nope. I wanted to see the guy who rode here in the ambulance, to thank him. Leo said he was waiting outside. Did you see him?"

In the sickly hospital light she thought she saw the big man flinch. He nodded with a ghost of his usual grin. "Yeah. Sorry to ruin your day, Genius, but that was me."

If she hadn't been afraid it would attract the attention of the big, mustachioed nurse, Genie would've groaned. Wellington? *Beef* Wellington had held her hand all the way to the hospital? And she had *liked* it? Had *vibrations?*

She muttered, "I think I need another CAT scan," and pulled the covers up over her face.

His dry chuckle sounded in the room and her stomach gave a little flutter. Probably from the concussion. "No you don't. Dr. Murphy says you'll be fine with a little rest. You're just embarrassed that you begged me to hold your hand and ride with you." His voice, mellow and warm, dropped a conspiratorial notch. "I won't tell if you don't."

She spluttered and yanked the covers back down, squinting in the overbright light. "I never begged."

"Suit yourself, Watson." Nick moved around the room with purpose, locating her clothes on a nearby stool and holding out the gray wool skirt that she never wanted to see again as long as she lived. "Get dressed, the doc says you can go home."

"I can?" Genie couldn't look at the skirt so she focused on his eyes, which were a warmer shade of blue than she remembered. Melting ice rather than a glacier. "He changed his mind?"

"Not exactly." Wellington looked down and noticed that the skirt was stiff with dried blood. He dropped it back on the pile and wiped his hands on his stained lab coat. "Never mind that. You can wear a blanket out. Want me to help you?"

"No, thank you." She didn't want his help. She didn't want his presence. She particularly didn't want him to see her zebra undies through the mile-wide slit in the back of the johnny.

But when she sat up, the room spun sickeningly and the honey rice cake she'd scarfed down between experiments that morning threatened a return visit.

"Easy there. I've got you, you're okay." His hands were steady on her shoulders and she sagged forward against his solid chest until she could feel his heartbeat against her cheek.

Suddenly her head didn't hurt so much anymore.

"I want to go home." She didn't care that she was whining, that there were tears in her voice. She wanted her condo. She wanted a shower. She wanted to be alone when the tears came.

"I know you do. We're going." His voice rumbled against her cheek and the room spun again as he gathered her, blankets and all, in his arms and lifted her as though she weighed no more than her kitten. She closed her eyes and pressed her face in the hollow between his jaw and shoulder, where the smell of soap and musk was strongest.

"Are you taking me to a cab?" She didn't think she had the strength to get herself out of a taxi and into her condo, but if that's what it took to reach her own bed, she'd find a way—even if it meant crawling up the stairs on her hands and knees with her safari underwear shining like a striped beacon out the back of the hospital johnny.

She thought he smiled, heard a thread of laughter

in his voice as he replied, "You're not getting rid of me that easily, Genius." The automatic doors whooshed open and she felt the change as they escaped from the hospital into the night air, crisp with fall in New England even through the funk of nearby Chinatown. "I'm taking you home."

THE WATCHER SAW A BIG MAN in a doctor's coat carry Dr. Watson past a row of busy ambulances toward the garage. She was wrapped in a blue blanket and from his vantage point deep in the darkness of a recessed stairwell, the watcher imagined her naked. He throbbed with frustration as he imagined what might have been. It should have been a warning for her. A pleasure for him.

His fingers rose to touch the neat bandage above his ear as desire turned to anger. The bitch had hurt him. She was going to pay for that.

Before, he'd merely wanted to stop her.

Now, he was going to end her.

Chapter Two

Nick left the blanket-wrapped woman asleep in his Bronco and unlocked the door to her home with keys he found in her practical canvas handbag. He started to make a quick check of the place, then slowed down as surprise rattled through him.

He wasn't sure what he'd expected Genie Watson's home to look like, but it sure as heck wasn't *this*.

At work, Dr. Genius was a petite woman, maybe five-four tops, a hundred pounds or so wet, with middling brown hair always pulled back in some twisty thing and a penchant for wearing shapeless clothing in shades of brown, black and beige. Nick had always thought that her eyes, big gray pools framed by thick lashes and high, sculpted cheekbones, were her best feature.

Now, having seen—and felt—firsthand how well she filled out those surprisingly bawdy underthings, he might have to reconsider.

He would have figured her living space to be along the same lines as her wardrobe—conservative, boxy rooms with sensible furniture decorated in shades of gray and brown, maybe with a touch of navy added in a wild moment that had since been regretted. He never would have pictured the spacious two-bedroom condo tucked into the eaves of an elegant Victorian only a few blocks from his place.

The four rooms on the first level flowed into each other like water, a river of golden wood floors, white trim and pastel walls. The huge windows were high and arched, topped by semicircles of abstract stained glass, and he imagined that daylight would splash crazily across the bold Indian rugs, the comfy, jewel-toned furniture and the dizzying array of dust collectors.

If Watson's constant complaints and annoying little memos hadn't told Nick everything he needed to know, her condo would've done the trick. The place practically screamed "a high maintenance woman lives here," and Nick'd had enough of them to last a lifetime and then some. In fact, he thought as he looked around again and scowled at the pretty stained-glass lamps, Lucille probably would've like this place—if it'd been three times bigger and ten times the price.

Well, he thought, no matter. He was here out of kindness, not interest, so it shouldn't matter to him that Watson was high-maintenance. He wasn't in the market for a relationship, and if he was, Genius Watson would rank somewhere around fifth from the bottom on the list of women he knew—with the ninety-year-old grandmother at the Chinese Laundromat right above her.

Scowling at the direction his thoughts had taken, which could only be excused by the bizarre events of the day, he returned to the Bronco to retrieve Dr. Watson. She didn't wake up when he carried her in and placed her on the plush cushions of an oversize couch, and he wondered fleetingly whether he should rouse her. He was pretty sure you weren't supposed to let a person with a concussion sleep all night.

It was too bad he hadn't thought to ask the fresh-faced intern for Watson's care-and-feeding instructions, but since the doctor wasn't going to spring her unless she'd had a medically trained observer to stay with her for at least twenty-four hours, Nick had snarled, "I'm a doctor. I'll watch her."

Well, he *was* a doctor. But courses in what to do after a concussion hadn't been required in the Biochem Department at M.I.T.

He could've left her where she was, but he remembered the day he'd broken his wrist in a Little League game. His parents had been at a fund-raiser, the nanny had been on vacation, and a private nurse wasn't available until the next day. So he'd stayed in the big hospital bed in an empty room far away from the rest of the children. He'd been ten years old. He'd been alone. And he'd hated every minute of it.

High-maintenance, memo-writing Genius Watson might not be his favorite person on a good day, but this counted as anything but a good day. His mind blinked to the sight of her in the developer room and his gut twisted. After an experience like that, even if she couldn't remember most of it, she deserved to spend the night in her own bed if that's what she wanted. From his eavesdropping in the hallway, he'd gotten the idea that she was firmly set on going home, so here he was, in a pretty condo with an even prettier woman asleep on the couch.

How had he overlooked Genie Watson's beauty before? Even with a rainbow of bruises marring her jaw and a line of stitches crawling across her right eyebrow, she was lovely. Her narrow, bruised hands rested beneath her left cheek and her even breathing tugged at a ringlet of her hair that had fallen from its customary twist. The surprisingly rich brownish-bronze glittered as it rippled over the patchwork quilt he'd found on the back of the sofa and thrown over her.

Nick supposed that he might have missed appreciating the delicate bones of her jaw when it was clenched in irritation because he'd forgotten the wipe tests again. He might not have noticed the pouting fullness of her lips when they were flapping at him for spilling stain on the UV projector or running the sterilizer too hot. But as Nick looked at Genius Watson now, he wondered how he ever could have dismissed her as ordinary. How he could have failed to look beyond the prickly gray wool and scratchy lace collars to see the woman beneath. Because, Lord, she was beautiful when she was unconscious.

It was too bad she'd wake up eventually.

''Wellington?'' Her soft voice jolted him back to reality. He'd been so busy staring at her, he'd missed that her eyes were open, cloudy with fatigue and pain. ''Why are you still here?''

He shrugged and tried to choke down the hot ball of…something that rose when she sat up on the couch and the quilt drifted down to her waist. The hospital gown slipped far off her shoulder, down to the creamy up slope of a breast the likes of which he never would have imagined hid beneath those awful clothes. She shifted again and the material dipped lower, baring the faintest hint of darker, nubbled flesh—

Get a grip, Wellington! The voice didn't sound like the Senator now, it sounded like a slightly hysterical version of Nick's own. *That breast is attached to Genius Watson. Remember her? The most overbearing, overbright, annoying female you've ever had the misfortune of sharing lab space with?*

The voice was right. He had to get a grip. He shook his head to clear it. The incident that afternoon must have shaken him more than he'd thought. That was the only rational explanation for his sudden interest in Dr. Genius's breasts.

"I—" He cleared his throat. "I had to promise the doc I'd stay, so you're stuck with me for the night unless there's someone else you'd rather I call."

She closed her eyes in pain, or perhaps annoyance. "No, but that doesn't mean you have to stay. Thanks for the ride home, but you can leave now. I'll be fine by myself."

Nick settled himself on the wide marshmallow of a love seat opposite her couch and linked his fingers behind his head. "I don't blame you for wanting some space, but I'd be going back on my word if I left you alone." He crossed his legs at the ankles. "Either I stay or you go back to Boston General. Got it?"

She frowned. "I said I'll be fine, Beef. I don't need your help."

"Nick," he corrected, ignoring the rest. "You call me Beef tonight and I'll take you back to the E.R. and tell the doctor that you seized and I think you need every sort of invasive, embarrassing test imaginable.''

''Fine. Nick. Whatever.'' She gave in with ill grace, struggled to her feet and swayed. ''I'm going to go take a shower.''

He held a hand out to steady her. Should've known she'd be a difficult patient. She'd never made anything easy for him before, why start now? He'd probably have been better off leaving her in the hospital. But no, as he watched her shiver in the warm, cozy living room, he knew he couldn't have done that.

Growing up, he had learned early and well that it was up to him to protect the people around him. And if ever in his life Nick had seen someone in need of protection, she was standing right in front of him, trying to look tough and self-reliant even though the kitten skulking behind the television could probably have knocked her over with one tiny paw.

Ever the politician's son, Nick chose his words carefully. He couldn't very well help her if she kicked him out on his ass. ''I don't think that's a good idea. What if you black out and hit your head again? Then it's back to the hospital and Nurse Mustache for sure.''

She shuddered and he saw a flash of vulnerability beneath the prickles—a confused, hurt woman looking out through Genius Watson's bruised eyes—and the image only strengthened his desire to help. ''I need a shower, Welling—uh, Nick. My brain may not be telling me what happened today, but my body remembers.'' She rubbed her arms and he noticed a series of marks on her shoulder, near her throat. Four bruises the size of a man's fingers.

He felt the anger boil low in his gut and hated the fact that an intruder had come into the lab and he hadn't done a thing to stop it. He should have sheltered the people he worked with. He should have been smarter. Faster. *Better.*

Genie shivered again, and Nick gave in to the urge to soothe. He touched her bruised cheek with the back of his hand, was surprised by the quick jolt that ran the length of his arm at the contact, and was even more surprised when the visible outline of a taut, peaked nipple showed through the thin hospital robe, mute testimony that she'd felt it, too.

Whoa there, he thought, trying to quell the quick thump of his libido. *Protect, remember? Protect, not ogle. You don't even like her. And besides, she's had a hell of a day. Leave her alone.* Figuring that his conscience had a point there, Nick took a deep breath and willed away the surprisingly compelling image of Dr. Genius wearing nothing but a lab coat. "Well…"

She frowned and the hurt moved to the back of those pretty gray eyes. "Don't give me grief on this, Wellington. In case you've forgotten, someone broke into Thirteen today and…ruined the developer." Her eyes darted to the shadows near the kitchen and she tapped her temple. "Whoever did it is up here— I saw him. I heard him. And I don't remember any of it. I *need* to remember it. Now, if you'll excuse me, I'm going to take a shower and I'd like a little privacy."

She tried to brush past him, but her grand exit was ruined when she wobbled on the first stair. Cursing under his breath, Nick grabbed her elbow just as she was about to lose her balance and half carried her up the stairs.

GENIE DISCOVERED THAT Wellington's version of privacy was far different from her own when he helped her into the shower, pulled the see-though butterfly curtain closed and waited for her to pass out the hospital johnny and the zebra underwear.

Her hands were shaking when she finally pointed the nozzle at the tiled wall while the water heated. She could see him standing by the sink, his broad shoulders and narrow hips made wavy by the plastic curtain, and she wondered what it was that she felt when he came near her. What were those warm vibrations that ran through her at his touch and made her snarl? Concussion, or something else?

Something impossible that jittered in her stomach and confused her. She, who was never, ever confused.

It had to be the circumstances, she told herself. She was still shaky, that was all. She'd been attacked— there, she'd said it—in her own lab. She could be excused for being shaky.

A tear cruised down her cheek and she didn't bother to brush it away.

When the water was hot, she turned it toward her chest, careful to keep the stitches dry. She'd wash her hair later, but for now she let the heavy stream of water beat down on her breasts and belly, washing away her attacker's unremembered touch and easing the soreness of the angry bruises at her hips and breasts.

As she touched one of the black marks, she asked

her brain, What happened? Who attacked me? Why? What had he hoped to gain?

Genie frowned in concentration and her temples throbbed as her mind bounced up against an implacable barrier.

It was no use. Frustrated and achy, she muttered a curse and looked through the rising steam. She couldn't concentrate with Wellington in the room. He was too distracting. Took up too much space. "You can leave now," she said, her voice echoing in the tiled bathroom. "I'll call you if I have any trouble in here."

She saw his masculine outline, blurred by the moist air and the ridiculous shower curtain, shift from one foot to the other. "Are you sure? You're not feeling dizzy or anything?"

What would he do if she were dizzy? Get in the shower and hold her up? Scrub her back? Wash her hair?

Protected from fear by the web of amnesia, her brain chose that moment to prod her with a mental note. *Get a date.* Suddenly, Genie could smell acrylamide and musk over the delicate perfume of Parisian soap, and she had a quick, improbable fantasy of Dr. Nicholas Wellington naked in the shower with her, his large, blunt fingertips massaging her scalp and taking the ache away. She imagined his big hands working in maddening circles, moving down her neck, across her shoulders, and down... She started to feel dizzy, but not in the way he'd meant.

He would press himself against her backside—

And push hard, grind against her in the bloodred

light while the developer clanked and groaned so loud that nobody could hear her muffled screams.

"What is it? Genie, what's wrong? Do you feel faint?" She must have made some noise, because suddenly he was in the shower holding her tight while the water blasted them both, quickly plastering the clothing against his hard, sculpted body.

He pulled the butterflies closed, making the shower into a warm, safe nest lit with bits of reflected color. There were blue butterflies, Genie saw as she stared at them rather than at the man who held her, and green and yellow ones that shone through with bright, warm light.

Not red and black. And the roar of the water pounding down on them was the shower, not the X-ray developer. But she was still cold. So cold.

"Genie!" His voice was sharper now, demanding an answer, bringing her back through the red-black mist. "Are you in pain? Do you want to go back to the hospital?"

"No," she managed to get out through chattering teeth, grateful for his arms around her, grateful when he turned the water even hotter to ease the chills that gripped her. "No, I remembered a little of what happened. Just a quick flash, that's all."

"That's enough." His words were clipped, but his eyes were steady when she looked up into them. His hands were gentle on her body as he seemed to wrap himself around her until she felt a little warmer. A little safer. He rocked her back and forth until her trembling eased a bit, and said quietly, "I'm sorry."

Lulled by the feel of the man against her, it took a moment for Genie to register the words. Then she said, "For what? You didn't grab me in the darkroom. Even *you* wouldn't go that far to get time on the sequencer." She'd meant the last as a weak joke, but fell silent when the words came out sharp, bitchy, the way they always did when she tried to talk to Beef Wellington, thirteenth floor hunk.

No wonder he hated working near her. She couldn't even say good morning without sniping at him. *Get a life*, her brain reminded her.

Yeah, easy for it to say. It was just too bad for her that of all the classes she'd aced over the years, she'd missed Get a Life 101. It had probably conflicted with calculus.

They stood there for a moment and Genie tried to frame an apology in her mind—one that sounded if not friendly at least less nasty. She shifted away from him, hoping that distance would bring more clarity to thoughts that seemed steeped in his heady scent. Instead the motion dragged the tips of her breasts across the wet material of his T-shirt and she froze as she became intimately, acutely aware that she was naked and he was not.

The small space within the butterfly curtain grew warmer and her breasts suddenly felt harder and softer at the same time, heavy with an unfamiliar, pulsing ache.

Over the pounding rush of the shower, she heard Wellington take a sharp breath. She looked up into his face and froze, mesmerized by the play of color and light across his features. The tendons of his strong neck stood out sharply beneath the slick skin of his throat, the muscles of his jaw rippled as he swallowed hard, and she wondered what he was thinking.

Was he wishing that he were anywhere but in the shower with Genius Watson? Was he thinking that his good deed for the day had turned into more of a project than he had planned? Was he thinking of the ride in the ambulance? Of the blood on her gray wool skirt and what might've happened if she hadn't fought back, hadn't been lucky?

Her eyes traveled up from his throat, slid across the wide planes of his cheekbones and up the aggressive jut of his nose to his eyes, which glittered through the steam like chunks of pale blue topaz. She wondered if maybe, just maybe, he was thinking the same thing she was thinking. Feeling the same things she was feeling.

Suddenly the events of the day didn't seem quite so unbelievable in the face of another incredible fact.

She was naked in the shower with Beef Wellington. She, Genius Watson, who in college had been voted by one mean-spirited fraternity as The Most Likely to Die a Virgin, was standing in the shower. Naked. With Nicholas Wellington III, the most popular, eligible, drop-dead gorgeous man at Boston General Hospital.

The wet material of his T-shirt grazed the hard tips of her breasts when he rasped in another breath and his soaked jeans were rough against her thighs and belly. She felt a liquid throb, warm and low, and her lips tingled with a phantom imprint as though he had kissed her already.

He sucked in a third breath as though filling his lungs was the most important thing in the world, then slid his hands up to cup her shoulders and Genie thought, *He feels it, too. He's going to kiss me.* Her

belly churned with a dizzying combination of antici-
pation, painkillers and delayed shock. She felt his fingers tighten, saw the muscles beneath the wet T-shirt
ripple, let her eyelids drift shut...

As he gently but firmly pushed her away, his eyes
glued to the nearest butterfly, he growled, "Since you
seem okay in here, I'm going to head downstairs and
dry off. Yell if you need my help." He practically
leaped out of the shower and was gone.

Genie sagged against the cool bath tiles and pressed
both hands to her burning cheeks once she heard the
bathroom door shut in his wake.

What had just happened here?

*You almost jumped Nick Wellington, that's what
happened,* her brain supplied as her heart stopped
pounding from excitement and started thumping from
sick, horrified embarrassment.

What had she been thinking?

She shook her head as the blasting inferno of—
lust? desperation? mental instability? delayed reaction?—slowly cooled and left her feeling nauseous.
She *hadn't* been thinking, which just showed what a
terrible day it had been. She *always* thought first and
acted second—it was the secret to an ordered, controlled life. A scientist's life.

A safe life.

Genie knew from experience that when she thought
through her actions she didn't make mistakes. Didn't
do stupid things. Didn't end up climbing out the third-
story window of a house on fraternity row with her
teeth chattering as sleet cut through her ripped shirt
and slicked the rose trellis beneath her numb fingers.

Pressing her bruised cheek to the tile, she made a

small sound of pain and frustration. Why could she remember every detail of that one humongous miscalculation during her college career and not a thing about this afternoon in the lab? Remembering her single date with Archer—gorgeous, popular, wealthy Archer—did her no good. It hadn't helped back then and it served no purpose now. But remembering what had happened in the darkroom was important. It could help Detective Sturgeon find the man who had attacked her. Could help hospital security figure out how he had gotten onto the locked thirteenth floor of Boston General's Genetic Research Building.

Might prevent it from—dear God—happening to someone else.

''Tell me!'' she ordered her brain, and tried to fight through the layers of defense to that blank place at the back of her mind. ''What happened, damn it? Who was it? Why?''

The fingermarks on her hips and breasts throbbed in time with her heartbeat, in time with the pounding of her head, but the blanks remained stubbornly blank except for a gentle California drawl and the phantom press of a man's fingers.

She closed her eyes and knew why Archer was suddenly vivid in her mind after more than a decade had passed. Her brain might not be willing to show her what had happened in the darkroom, but it wanted her to remember that she'd been stupid about men before. Really stupid.

''I get it, I get it,'' she muttered. ''Wellington's out of my league. You think I don't know that?'' She reached for the bar of expensive soap her mother sent her each month from Paris in an attempt to forge the connection they'd never managed when they lived on the same continent. "Besides, I don't even like him."

But she knew, as she slicked the soap over her breasts and down again, that for the first time in a long, long while she was lying to herself.

NICK PULLED A BEER out of the fridge—who would've guessed Dr. Genius drank beer?—and drained half of it while he stood at the sink and waited for his hands to stop shaking with a potent combination of lust and self-loathing.

What had he been thinking?

The answer was obvious. He hadn't been thinking. At least not with his brain. He closed his eyes and swore while the feel of her rocketed through his system and set off every warning buzzer in his body.

In a hundred years or so he might get past seeing Genie Watson lying in a pool of blood next to the smashed developer. But he was never, ever, going to forget the sight of her naked body, wet with the shower and glowing with reflected butterflies that filtered through the plastic curtain. And the feel of her. He cursed. It had taken every ounce of willpower he'd possessed to set her aside and to leave the shower while he still could. And it had been a close call at that.

He'd almost kissed a woman who'd been sexually attacked not eight hours earlier—that knowledge was enough to make him feel like a jerk. And the fact that the woman in question was Genius Watson…well, that was just downright scary.

Hadn't he learned anything from Lucille?

He chugged the rest of the beer in self-defense and

it went straight to his head, reminding him that he'd been too caught up in DNA sequencing to eat lunch and he'd spent dinnertime in the E.R. waiting room.

Since he absolutely wasn't going to follow up on any of the irrational suggestions his hormones were sending him, he decided to cook.

Food was the next best thing.

He heard the water being shut off upstairs while he peered into her refrigerator. Pleased that she was well stocked with food as well as beer, he decided on scrambled eggs and toast, making the meal heartier by adding onions, parsley, and a wedge of crumbly cheddar. He felt himself unwind a bit, relaxed by the mindless snick of the knife against the cutting board and the mundane pleasure of preparing a meal.

Mrs. Greta had taught him well. The Senator's cook had been a round, motherly woman who'd given her employer's growing son a swat or a hug depending on the circumstances, and some of Nick's happiest memories from back then were set in the rambling kitchen with her off-key humming in the background. She'd taught him to cook and hadn't told his father, for which Nick had been eternally grateful.

With the memory of the older woman bustling warm and happy around the edges of his mind, Nick breathed deeply through his nose and looked up toward the second floor, wishing idly that he could see through the walls to the steamy shower beyond. If he closed his eyes, he was sure he could picture Genie Watson in glorious, pink-wet nakedness....

With a man's fingerprints glowing purple against the rosy skin. The marks of violence at her neck, hips and face. A crumpled white ball under the chemical sink. A pool of blood, dried black at the edges, liquid and dark red in the center.

The housekeeper's happy ghost vanished and Nick scowled at a half-peeled onion. He was here because a co-worker had been attacked. Because she had wanted to come home and needed someone to stay with her.

Someone to protect her.

He slid the mixture into a skillet while his thoughts poked and prodded at the facts. The detective, Sturgeon, had said there was no reason to think that Genie had been the target, but it didn't make much sense to picture someone hiding in the darkroom waiting to assault the first person that walked in. Then again, picturing someone hiding in the darkroom didn't make any sense at all to begin with.

Why their lab? Why the darkroom? How the hell had he gotten onto a locked floor in the first place? And how had he gotten away?

At the thought of a blood-covered, would-be rapist escaping through his lab space, and what might have happened had Genie not defended herself, Nick missed an English muffin with a wickedly serrated bread knife and almost took off his own thumb. "Shi-oot!"

"Be careful. I'm a little too shaky to sew you back together and I'm not up for another trip to the emergency room tonight, okay?"

Sucking on the narrow slice he'd carved into his thumb, Nick looked up to see Genie, wrapped in a thick terry robe, standing at the threshold. Her hair was a damp waterfall across her narrow shoulders. Her eyes were shadowed, wary, and the bruises on her cheek forcibly reminded him of her vulnerability even as his heart thumped at the sight of her. She needed his help, nothing more. His protection. Besides, he didn't even like her.

"You cook?" Her voice was stronger, as if the shower had distanced her from the afternoon's events, and he was grateful for that, since he wasn't feeling particularly distant himself. In fact, he was fighting the insane urge to cross the room, scoop her off her feet and take her back to the shower so he could protect her. Naked.

"Yeah, I cook." He waved the thumb in her direction. "If you don't mind the occasional miss." Giving her a wide berth, he placed two plates on the granite breakfast bar that separated the kitchen from the dining area.

"But I thought—" She hitched herself up on a stool, seeming not to notice that the robe had fallen open across one rosy, damp thigh.

Resisting the urge to pull the robe closed—or off, whichever she preferred—he sat opposite her so he couldn't see her pink-painted toenails. Never in a million years would he have guessed that Genius Watson painted her toenails pink.

"What? That a rich boy like me wouldn't know how?" He shrugged. "Well, when you get along better with the help than with your own family, you pick up a few useful domestic skills."

Most women would choose that moment to comment on his father's wealth and position, or ask him what the campaign had been like. Genie did neither. She popped a forkful of egg into her mouth, made a sexy "Mmm" sound when she swallowed and said, "Poor baby. Do you do windows, too?"

He relaxed the tension he hadn't even realized had crept into his neck and shoulders, bit into the toast and nodded toward the full-length windows surrounding the ground floor. "Yeah, but I'd charge you extra for those, particularly if you wanted me to polish the stained glass."

"I'll keep that in mind." After a few minutes of oddly companionable silence, she stared at her empty plate. "I guess I was hungry. Thanks."

He got up and dished out seconds, grateful that she was lucid and eating. He added a couple of prescription pain pills and a glass of water to her place setting before he sat back down.

She scowled at the pills. "They'll knock me out. I need something that won't make my brain fuzzy."

Without a word he leaned across the breakfast bar and grabbed the ibuprofen he'd put there earlier, popped the cap and handed it to her. "Kind of thought you'd feel that way."

She swallowed four of the pills dry and chased them with a bite of egg. Gesturing again with her fork, oblivious to the fact that her terry robe was now gaping at the top, she said, "So what happened? I don't remember much, but the darkroom was trashed, wasn't it?"

Nick tore his attention from the hint of smooth, round flesh at her widening neckline and glued his eyes to her face, which was looking worse by the minute as the bruises darkened to the color of rotten eggplants. *Protect,* he reminded himself, *not ogle.* "Yeah, the cassettes were opened and the films thrown around, and it looks like he went after the developer with that pipe wrench we use to change the chemical tanks. He, uh, must've done that before you got there.''

''How do you know that?'' She grimaced and pushed her plate aside.

''Well, from the amount of—'' Nick cleared his throat and willed the image away ''—blood on you and in the room, he'd have been too hurt to demolish anything afterward.''

Genie shook her head and her drying hair shimmered in the light of the stained-glass lamp. How had he ever thought her hair was a nondescript brown? The metallic threads of bronze and gold glowed as she moved, and the natural waves washed almost to the place where her breasts pushed against the rapidly loosening terry robe.

Ordinary she was not. But that didn't change the fact that she was a pain in the neck.

''That doesn't make any sense. I would've known something was wrong if the developer wasn't running properly. And besides, how did he just waltz back down the hallway, onto the elevator, and past security? Wouldn't someone have thought it strange? I mean, sure it's a hospital, but bleeding people tend to stick to the E.R., not the research buildings.

She had a point. ''Well, there was blood in the sink. Maybe he washed some of it off.'' Nick closed his eyes and tried to picture the ruined room. What was he missing? ''How about clothes? A lab coat or something he could've put on over his other stuff? A baseball cap to cover a scalp wound?''

''A scalp wound would work,'' Genie agreed, her

eyelids drooping and her words coming more slowly now. "It'd bleed like hell but not do too much real damage. The clothes make sense, but where would he get them? Bring them with him? Why would he do that unless he was planning on getting hurt? And why was he in there in the first…" She trailed off and would have fallen asleep face-first in her leftover eggs if Nick hadn't seen it coming and reached over to catch her chin in his hand.

Why indeed?

He stared at her face, at the translucent skin, the bloom of violent bruises, the obscene line of black stitches above her swollen eye. She looked like an angel who'd gotten the losing end of a bar fight. Why would anyone want to hurt her? Hurt their research? They found disease genes, for heaven's sake. They didn't clone dinosaurs, they didn't work with embryos and they didn't use lab animals in their experiments.

They tried to cure people. Why would anyone want to hurt researchers who were only trying to cure people?

Nick had no idea. Nor, it seemed, did either of the detectives working on the case. At least not yet.

Sighing, he picked up Dr. Watson and manfully rearranged her robe so it covered as much as possible. He carried her up the spiral staircase to her bedroom, flicked on a faux Tiffany lamp that lit the room in bits of sparkling color and laid her on the big brass bed. She didn't wake when he slid her between the covers and tucked them all the way up to her chin, but she murmured and curled up with both hands beneath her cheek.

Her two cats, which he had previously noticed only

as flitting shadows at the edge of vision, appeared on the bed as if by magic. The big black shorthair curled itself behind her knees and the tiny gray tabby, maybe two months old or so, purred like a locomotive as it marched up to her face and sniffed at the line of stitches. It licked her chin worriedly.

The kitten looked directly at Nick and mewed a question. He stroked its little head with the back of a finger, and said, "Yeah, I hear you. She'll be okay though." He stared down at the motionless woman, barely a lump beneath the bedclothes. "She'll be okay," he repeated. "I'll protect her."

He paused and said to nobody in particular as he stared down at the woman in the bed, "I'll protect her. God help us both."

Chapter Three

While Genie slept, her brain, that precocious organ that had dictated much of her life up until this point, churned and spun in its liquid-filled housing and tried to make sense of the day's events. A difficult task considering there was a large piece of that day tucked away in the back recesses of memory, protected by a twist of neurons and a few subconscious Keep Away signs.

She frowned; her sleeping self registering the pain of pulled stitches and ordering her face muscles to relax even as her dreams flickered red and black.

She had gone to the developer room, excited to read the films from the day before. They were about to begin analysis of a new Gray's Glaucoma family and she wanted to see how the DNA samples were working, particularly since Molly had gotten a strange phone call from the family's wealthy patriarch the day before.

The old man might just be a tube of DNA to the lab rats, but to the rest of the world he was a tycoon. A powerhouse. Someone that Genie wanted to keep very, very happy in the hopes that he'd donate generously to the Eye Center's new wing. She made a mental note to return his call and be extra nice.

Placing a hand on the exterior port, she assured herself that the developer was running properly. The tray was hot to the touch, a puff of air ran across its surface to keep the films from sticking to the hard plastic, and the hallway was filled with the sound of turning rollers.

She glanced over the new cartoon taped to the wall near the darkroom door and a faint smile touched her lips. Dr. Nicholas Wellington might be a big, handsome jerk with no sense of protocol and an annoying habit of appropriating her equipment just when she needed it most, but his arrival had given the lab a certain sense of character. She glanced at his office door and grinned at a poster that featured a buff body with a cutout picture of Wellington's head taped in place, the caption reading, Is This The Face Of Erectile Dysfunction? followed by an eight-hundred number for one of those new potency drugs.

Shaking her head, Genie grinned wider. Though she highly doubted that Wellington suffered from E.D., she had to give him points for leaving the poster where his techs had hung it.

He either had a great sense of humor or he was, so to speak, awfully cocky about his abilities.

Reassured that the developer was running, she reached for the spinning door and rotated it so she could step into the darkroom without letting in any white light. As she entered the light lock, she was surprised to see that the Occupied sign was lit. She sniffed. Wellington. She banged on the back of the light lock. "My turn, Beef. Check the chart!"

But there was no response. Maybe he'd left the sign lit after he was done. Genie snorted. Slob. She tried calling his name again before she entered the light lock, heard the *rubba-thump, rubba-thump* of the revolving door as she let herself into the darkroom—

She was in a field of daisies. Her cat, Oddjob, sat at her feet while Galore gamboled through the flowers, leaping in huge bounds to see over the stalks while he swatted at the yellow and black butterflies with kitten's paws.

In her sleep Genie cried out in frustration at her brain's refusal to show her what had happened in the darkroom. She twisted against the bedclothes and whimpered when she brushed a clenched fist against the ripe bruise on her cheek. Then The Voice returned and she stilled.

"Shh, sweetheart, it's only a dream. You're safe. I'm here."

She struggled against sleep again, fighting to wake to tell him that she wasn't afraid of the dream, that she was frustrated by the missing pieces. But the bed dipped as he settled beside her and she felt a whisper of a touch at her forehead that took away the pain. She sighed and snuggled deeper, turning her bruised cheek into his hand.

"Sleep now. I'll keep watch."

In the field, the cats purred and Genie turned her face up into the warm yellow sunlight. She felt Nick behind her and knew if she turned her head she'd see him, larger than life and twice as handsome—the high Viking cheeks, the flat blade of a nose and the warm blue eyes. But as she moved, something else caught her eye, a flash of mossy color at her shoulder. She looked down—

And saw that she was wearing green scrubs stained brown with blood.

"GREENS," GENIE PRONOUNCED the next morning, waving a forkful of strawberry pancake in Nick Wellington's direction before popping it into her mouth. It sure beat a handful of granola on the way out the door. *If Wellington sticks around,* she thought, *I'll have to exhume the StairMaster from the attic.*

"Excuse me?"

She dropped her fork onto the plate with a loud clatter and blushed before she realized he hadn't heard her slip of the medulla. And where had *that* come from? There was no way Nick Wellington was sticking around. No way she wanted him to. In the cold, rational light of morning, that little incident in the shower seemed like an out-of-body experience, like something that had happened to someone else. Now it was—hopefully—time for them to get back to reality.

Back to Dr. Genius Watson and Dr. Beef Wellington. Matter and antimatter. Magnetic north and south. It would serve her well to remember that, because there was no way in hell she was making the Archer mistake twice.

Besides, Wellington wasn't even interested. Sure he'd felt sorry for her, and maybe a tiny bit responsible because he'd found her. Nothing more. He certainly hadn't felt the hum of rightness in the ambulance and he hadn't been prey to the fantasies she'd briefly entertained in the night.

He couldn't have, or else he wouldn't have bolted from the shower as if she had just grown a third eyeball in the center of her forehead. She had been naked—*naked!*—in his arms and her breasts had been rubbing up against his wet T-shirt and her thighs and her— Well, never mind. Genie resisted an unladylike snort. He hadn't done a thing. He hadn't kissed her, hadn't even made a suggestive comment.

Nothing.

Ergo, he wasn't interested. It didn't take a genius to figure that one out. And it was just as well, she thought, since she absolutely, positively, wasn't interested, either.

Screw me once, said Marilynn's well-bred, Georgian contralto in the back of Genie's mind, *shame on you. Screw me twice...* Genie's lips twitched. She was pretty sure the conclusion of Marilynn's malaprop didn't really apply here, but it felt good to remember her friend, as if Marilynn's ghost was standing at her shoulder, protecting her from being stupid.

"Genie?" Nick waved his hand in front of her face. "You still here?"

She mumbled something unintelligible while she tried to remember what they'd been talking about. Oh, yeah. "Greens," she repeated and he nodded.

"That's what I thought you said. Are we talking about lettuce, kale, spinach, that sort of thing?" He sipped at the coffee, which had turned out fragrant, flavorful and perfect, three things she had thought totally beyond her Mr. Coffee.

"No, greens as in surgical scrubs. I dreamed about them last night."

Wellington looked at her as if that was the worst

possible thing he could think to dream about, which it probably was. She bet he dreamed Technicolor fantasies starring tall blondes with chest measurements roughly equivalent to their IQs.

"So?"

She leaned forward. "That's how he got out of the darkroom. My greens. I keep a set in there for changing the developer chemicals. What do you want to bet they're not there anymore?"

Genie smiled when he nodded agreement, and was surprised to feel the tension across her shoulders loosen a little. Talking to Wellington over pancakes seemed to be making the events of the day before a little more bearable. A little less awful.

Not smart, her brain supplied, *remember Archer.* And she did. She remembered Archer in all his golden, popular glory. He might not have broken her heart, but he'd certainly shattered her pride.

"Yeah, that sounds reasonable. I'll mention it to the detectives when I see them later today."

Nick stood and piled his dishes in the sink before he grabbed his keys off the breakfast bar. Genie wondered fleetingly why he'd left them there when there was a perfectly good key rack just inside the door. Then she sighed. It was a timely reminder of their differences. She had racks, he had piles.

Magnetic north and south. She'd do well to remember it.

"I'm going to run an errand or two, check in at the lab and speak with the detectives. You going to be okay?"

So that was it, then. Genie tried to ignore the faint sadness that trickled through her. "Sure, I'll be fine.

My car's parked in Chinatown so I'll catch a cab to the commuter rail.''

He paused halfway out the door. ''You're not planning on going to work today, are you?''

Though the very thought of it made her queasy, she said, ''Of course I am.''

He blew out a slow breath and abandoned subtlety. ''You were beat up yesterday, Genie. You've got stitches in your eyebrow and I can tell your head's killing you. Can't you take the day off?''

Sure she could, but she didn't want to. Already the idea of taking the elevator up to their shared floor and walking past the developer room was filling Genie with prickles of dread. She knew it would only get worse the longer she stalled. Her brain might be filling the emptiness with irrelevant thoughts of Nick Wellington in her shower and annoyingly apropos mental notes, but her soul knew the truth.

A big, tough guy like Wellington might not understand, but she was scared. Deep-down, bone-thumping scared.

What if the man was still in the darkroom? What if he'd hidden in the little office closet where she kept a change of clothes? She could feel him looking over her shoulder right now, breathing on her neck; the bruises on her stomach ached when she shivered.

What if the police found him near the lab and he told them that he'd been watching her for weeks, just waiting for his chance?

Or even worse, what if they didn't find him at all? Would she spend the rest of her life trying to remember him, jumping at every shadow that might remind her of what she couldn't know? Or would she remember him one day, remember what he had said, what he had done.

And wish that she could forget it again.

She shivered and rubbed an absent hand across a sore spot on her neck. "I could stay home, but I don't want to." Her self-appointed guardian scowled and she frowned right back. "I need to walk into that lab today, Wellington. I need to prove to myself that I can go back there and function." She paused. "Otherwise he's taken away more than just my feeling of safety. He's taken away the lab."

And although Wellington would have no way of knowing it, the lab was more than just a workplace to Genie. It was her life. Her salvation.

Her world.

He sighed and nodded. When he scrubbed a hand down the golden stubble on his jaw, Genie noticed for the first time that he looked tired. Worn. And very sexy in a grumpy, I'm-wearing-yesterday's-clothes kind of way.

"Okay," he said, "I can understand that. But let me drive you. I'm going to swing by my place." He named a nearby section of town, surprising her. She hadn't realized they were almost neighbors. "Once I've changed, I'm going to take care of a few things, then I'll come back here and get you. Okay?"

He nodded and scratched the stubble on his jaw, clearly satisfied with his own plan. Taking lack of disagreement for an agreement, he gave her shoulder a friendly squeeze and left. The condo seemed much bigger and emptier in his absence.

Her shoulder tingled where he had touched it.

And the silence was as loud as a thousand freezer alarms shrieking at once.

Genie shivered. She was alone. Beef Wellington and his space-hogging tendencies were gone. There was no one else here. She was alone. The shadows seemed to pulse with it.

"Get over it, Watson," she ordered herself. "You've been on your own for a long time and it hasn't hurt you yet."

Yet, throbbed the bruises on her breasts and belly as her brave words echoed through the silent space. She shivered again, suddenly sure that there were eyes in the empty darkness of the hallway beyond the kitchen.

What if he knew where she lived?

"Prr-meow?"

Genie jumped a mile and the kitten skittered away. She forced a little laugh. That was why she kept pets, after all. For those times when the quiet was too loud.

"Meep?" Galore inquired again, and set her miniature claws in the jeans Genie had pulled on that morning, unwilling to face Nick in her robe again. He'd been in the kitchen already and had dispelled any awkwardness between them by serving her breakfast, checking her pupils, and not mentioning her nightmares or the man-size imprint on her bed.

Looking at the jeans, she muttered, "Hell with it. I'm going casual," and slid off the bar stool, slinging the limp kitten over her shoulder where it buzzed contentedly.

She couldn't bear the thought of her usual work clothes—professional, grown-up, boring, the kind of things she'd originally chosen to make herself seem older. Now it was a habit, though she often wished she could wear her jeans and soft cashmere turtlenecks to the lab, and dreamed of leaving her hair long, or tucking it back in a simple braid that made her look carefree.

Young.

Maybe even pretty? said a soft Georgian accent in the back of her head. Genie shook her head with a half smile. Marilynn always had been an optimist.

"Hell with it," she muttered again. "I'm wearing jeans today. I deserve it." She was sore and grumpy and the thought of French-twisting her hair over the bump on the back of her head was enough to make her scream. She pulled a soft bra over her head and scowled at the bruises on her arm and stomach. "Bastard."

She was going to find out who had wrecked the developer room and she was going to make him pay. Her brain was going to help her whether it wanted to or not. She was going to figure out what had happened and why—and if she had to go right through handsome Nick Wellington and his pat-the-little-lady-on-the-head-and-leave-her-at-home-while-the-big-strong-man-talks-to-the-police attitude, then so be it.

Chapter Four

She hadn't waited for him. Of course she hadn't. Nick scowled as he jammed the Bronco into a miniscule space between two identical minivans on the Massachusetts Turnpike. One of the drivers swerved, honked and made a rude gesture that was immediately picked up by the toddler in the back.

Nick ignored them and took the off ramp to Boston General's parking garage, just outside the theater district. He didn't know why he was surprised. Any woman who skipped pain pills in favor of a few puny aspirin when she had a face full of stitches and a concussion would be unlikely to sit tamely at home waiting to be picked up.

Of course she'd called a cab.

Nick locked the Bronco and jogged down the cement staircase to exit the garage. Though the hospital had built a series of catwalks and connecting tunnels to allow its employees to move from building to building without venturing outside, Nick preferred the quarter-mile hike through Chinatown. It added an interesting variety of smells to his day.

As he walked, he pondered Genie's defection until

he had to laugh at himself. When he stopped to buy a soda from a street vendor, he finally admitted the truth.

He was disappointed, darn it.

He'd wanted to drive in with her. He wanted to be sure she was okay, wanted to walk into the lab together in case the memory came crashing back all at once. In case it didn't. Sure, they'd never gotten along particularly well before, but there was a first for everything. Maybe this horrible incident would have a positive side. Maybe they could call a truce. Find some common ground.

Take another shower.

Wincing at the thought of her reaction if he ever suggested such a thing, Nick swiped his passkey for admittance into BoGen's Genetic Research Building, stepped through the sliding door—

And froze when he saw Detective Sturgeon standing in the lobby surrounded by most of the researchers, interns and techs who worked on the thirteenth floor. Genie wasn't among them.

Nick's heart thundered in his ears as he crossed the lobby with quick strides. Her attacker had come back to finish the job. Watson had been hurt, raped, or worse.

"What happened?" he practically yelled.

A babble of voices erupted as, excited, each of the techs tried to answer at once. The words "spill," "gel boxes" and "radiation safety Nazis" filtered out of the hubbub and Nick relaxed a fraction as he called the elevator.

"Jared, keep everyone down here until I call down with the all clear, okay?" The tech grimaced and nodded. The chain that dangled from his pierced nostril swung from side to side at the motion.

Then the elevator arrived and Nick took a deep breath and told himself to relax as the car began to move. Genie was fine. It was just a radioactive spill. A serious but containable lab incident that had nothing to do with the previous day's events in the darkroom.

Or did it?

UNTIL NICK ARRIVED, Genie hadn't known she'd been waiting for him. But when he stepped over the yellow Caution/Radioactive tape and joined her in the little room where they ran the DNA separating gels, she felt the tension drain from her in waves and had the insane urge to throw her arms around his waist and blubber while he dealt with Dixon and plied her with painkillers for her headache.

Since that probably would have horrified him, she didn't. But she thought about it. That is, until he looked down at her, grinned and said, "Hey, baby, you new here?"

She rolled her eyes. "Shut up, Wellington."

He pretended surprise, but his perfect teeth flashed. "Why, Dr. Watson. Is that you? I didn't recognize you for a moment."

He meant because of the big, ugly bruises on her cheek and the stitches crawling across her forehead like a mutant Gypsy moth caterpillar. Genie didn't want to cry on him anymore—she wanted to punch him. She knew she looked terrible. He didn't have to rub it in. He'd made it plain enough the night before that he didn't consider her desirable. She sighed and jammed her hands into her jeans pockets. Oh, well.

Beef Wellington didn't want her.

Big surprise.

Resisting the urge to whistle cheerfully at the mutinous look on Genie's face, Nick asked, "What did you do, nuke the whole darn floor? That's not like you, Dr. Watson." He watched with feigned interest as George Dixon and his minions crawled around the room with absorbent cloths, Geiger counters and bottles of Count-Off, a nifty solution that washed away radioactive liquids. "It looks like we're having a rad safety party."

He kept his attention fixed on the moon-suited men because otherwise he might have swept Genie up in his arms, carried her to one of their offices—he wasn't particular about which one—and peeled away that clinging blue top and those skintight old jeans until she was naked in his arms. Again.

Madness.

She looked great with her hair untwisted and her swervy little body showcased in tight denim and soft blue. She looked younger, and Nick took a moment to wonder how old she was. He'd always figured her to be five or six years his senior, given her conservative clothes and double degree. But looking at her now, he reconsidered.

Then he remembered a mountain of memos and a prettily decorated condo and he summoned a scowl. It didn't matter how old she was. He hadn't been interested yesterday, and he wasn't interested today. One shower wasn't enough to wash away all his good sense.

"Ahem." An officious cough brought Nick's attention back to the gel room.

George Dixon, dictator of the radiation safety department, stretched to his full height—still two inches shorter than a slouching Nick—and glared. "No party, Wellington. I could shut you two down for this." He gestured around the small room. "Radioactive buffer spilled in here, contaminated towels scattered in the main room, incomplete marking of used vials, and—" He paused for emphasis before pronouncing the most dire of sins. "You're a week behind in your wipe tests."

Nick turned toward Genie and rolled his eyes. Their radiation use was well within acceptable bounds and Dixon knew it. He just liked to swing his... Geiger counter around.

Unfortunately, since Leo refused to listen to Nick's repeated complaints, Dixon had the power to do exactly as he threatened—shut down both labs based on minor infractions. So Nick laid a hand on Genie's shoulder and said, "Well, Dixon, I was on my way to do those wipe tests yesterday when, well, you know…"

Genie glared at him. She'd nagged him about those tests—an annoying and unnecessary procedure Dixon had initiated strictly to torture the labs—the middle of the previous week and Nick had promised to do them then.

However, the ploy worked. Dixon's expression switched from righteous indignation to concern. "I heard what happened to Genie. It's awful. Just terrible that someone could break into one of our buildings and do such a thing. Of course, I spoke to the police yesterday afternoon—somebody apparently told them of that little…misunderstanding between us a few months ago.'' He reached towards Genie. ''I was going to call you last night, but…''

She made a face and avoided his hand. ''There was no misunderstanding, George, except maybe you not grasping the meaning of 'stop calling me at home.''' She glanced at Nick. ''By 'misunderstanding,' he means 'restraining order.' George here believes in pursuing his lady friends, whether they like it or not.''

Dixon's response to that was muffled as he pulled his safety suit off and Nick felt a quick, predatory quiver. ''Hey, Dixon—what'd you do to your head?''

The other man put a hand to the neat bandage just under the hairline by his right ear. ''Racquetball. We were playing doubles and I caught a paddle in the head. Hurt like hell.'' He smirked at Nick. ''But don't go getting any crazy ideas, Wellington. Like I said, I've already talked to the police…and given them my alibi.''

SEVERAL HOURS LATER, once Dixon and his cronies had pronounced the area clean, packed up and left, Genie tried to get back to work. She failed miserably. Not because she lacked motivation—with the last two days' experiments ruined, she was desperate to get back to work before she fell horribly behind. And not because she was freaked out to be in her office. Thankfully, once she'd battled down her nerves enough to take the elevator upstairs, she'd found the rest of her return surprisingly easy.

Her head tech, Molly, and her clinical coordinator, Stephanie, had been surprised to see her, but quickly figured out that Genie's plan was to drown her lingering fear in work. So they'd scraped together the last two weeks' worth of developed films and dumped them on her desk. She was grateful and suddenly too busy to think about the revolving door down the hall that was still cordoned off with yellow police tape.

No, it wasn't lack of work or lingering jitters slowing her down. It was the amateur Sherlock Holmes in her office with one perfect butt cheek hitched on her desk and a pair of muscled arms—where did a biochemist get arms like that?—crossed across his equally well-defined chest.

"You should have waited for me this morning," he stubbornly maintained. "How many fingers am I holding up?" He waved a hand in her face and she scowled and batted it away.

"Eighteen. Lighten up, Be—uh, Nick. I'm fine."

He didn't seem convinced. "Well, the Dr. Watson we all know and love—" now *that* was a gross overstatement if ever she'd heard one or she wouldn't have escaped her shower unmolested "—would hardly come to work in…" He glanced at her legs. "Casual clothes. Nor would she be involved in a radioactive spill that threatened both our labs."

She'd ignore his reference to her disheveled looks, but there was no way she was letting him get away with accusing her of carelessness. She flared, "I wouldn't go there if I were you, Wellington. Which one of us has been responsible for the last *five* radioactive violations on this floor?"

Okay, so three of them had come on a single day, when Nick had made the mistake of laughing at

Dixon's very new, very expensive, very odd haircut, but who was counting?

"And besides," she continued, "the spill was an accident."

"Was it?" he countered. "How can you be sure?"

Genie felt an intensification of the uneasy niggling that had fluttered in her stomach ever since Molly had called her in to view the accident. "What else could it be?"

Nick shrugged. "Sabotage?" Then he snorted and shook his head. "Never mind, I must be tired because that doesn't make a whole lot of sense, does it?" But he still wished Sturgeon hadn't left. The guy might look like a fish, but he seemed to know his stuff.

Last night the detective had suggested that the attack was random, but Nick wasn't so sure. Sneaking into a research building and ambushing someone in a darkroom seemed like a lot of trouble to go to for a few sick jollies, particularly with Boston's red light district, the Combat Zone, nearby.

One thing was for sure—Nick was sticking close to Genie Watson until he was positive she was safe. This time he'd be smarter. Faster. Better.

He'd protect her. And to do that, he had to figure out what was going on. And he knew right where he wanted to start—with her ex-boyfriend. He'd never liked the rad-safety geek, but the surge of anger he'd felt when Dixon reached for Genie had been totally out of proportion. His gut was telling him something.

"What happened between you and Dixon?"

Genie winced and felt a faint blush rise. "Nothing much."

Nick nodded, clearly unconvinced. "Do you often

take out restraining orders against people who don't do anything to you?''

"No, of course not." She paused, but when Nick raised one eyebrow and tapped the place behind his ear where Dixon's bandage had been, she sighed and continued. "We dated. Briefly, and to my everlasting regret." There was no need to tell Wellington she'd gone out with Dixon simply because he'd asked and she was lonely. She'd soon figured out that there were worse things than being lonely.

"Did he say something that scared you? Did he do something?" Nick rubbed an impatient hand through his overgrown buzz cut. "Come on, Genie, give me a little help here. I know he says he has an alibi, but…"

She shook her head. "No, it was nothing like that. George was…clingy. Insistent. He wouldn't go away when I said I didn't want to see him anymore. He kept saying we had a deeper connection and that I shouldn't deny it." When Nick's eyes sharpened, she held up a hand. "Not in a creepy, violent way, though. I just don't see him as being involved in this."

"Why the hell not? The guy admits he's obsessed and you don't think it's even a remote possibility that he might've tackled you in the darkroom yesterday?" Nick swore and paced her office, not getting very far because it was crammed with journals and X-ray films. "He has a passkey, for God's sake. He could've just waltzed in and out and nobody would've thought anything of it!"

Genie closed her eyes as her headache kicked up a notch. Wellington just didn't understand. She'd gotten the restraining order to prove to George that she was serious about not seeing him, not because she was afraid. In a way, she was more like Dixon than she was like Wellington. George was a little strange and a lot lonely, and Wellington was...

Well, he was Wellington. And people like Wellington didn't understand people like Genie and George.

"He said he had an alibi," she repeated tiredly. "And if you're going to pace, go do it somewhere else. I have a headache."

She was spared his answer when the phone rang. Waving Nick out of her office, she picked up the receiver. She didn't bother to scowl when he ignored her gesture and plonked himself in a chair while she said, "Boston General Genetics Testing Unit, Dr. Watson speaking."

"Ah, Doctor! Just the person I was hoping to reach." The voice was rich and cultured, with the requisite touch of old Yankee to it. "This is Richard."

Nick mouthed, *Is it Sturgeon?* When Genie shook her head in the negative, he grabbed a gene therapy journal and started reading it, last page first.

"Yes, sir, it's lovely to hear from you!" Belatedly, Genie remembered that she had meant to return the wealthy patriarch's call the day before, but other things—such as a trip to the E.R.—had intervened. "What can I do for you?"

The old man harrumphed. "Well, I wanted to talk to you about that new wing your hospital is building for the Eye Center..."

They spoke for a few minutes about the sizable

donation he'd promised, then before he hung up, Richard mentioned the DNA study he and his family had just joined—the Gray's Glaucoma project.

"Have all of those children and grandchildren of mine given you what you need?"

Genie grinned into the phone. She had a feeling the old man ruled his extended family with an iron fist. "Now, Richard, you know that sort of information is strictly confidential. If you want to know anything about the other people in the study, you'll have to ask them." Genie noticed that Nick had flipped through all the advertisements at the back of the journal and was in the process of reading a cloning article from back to front.

The man on the phone harrumphed again, neither conceding nor arguing the point. "So have you run any tests on my family yet? Find anything?"

"No," Genie said slowly. She had thought Richard understood the releases he'd signed when he donated blood for the Gray's Glaucoma study. "It's too soon for any results. You do understand that I can't share ongoing results with you, right, Richard? That would be a breach of my ethics and my responsibility as a researcher."

"Of course, young lady. Of course." He paused tellingly. "But before you make any final decisions, think long and hard about your Eye Center, won't you? And then you can phone me back." The line went dead.

Genie stared at the phone for a good long minute.

"Something wrong?"

She glanced up at Nick and shook her head. "Not really. Just a study participant." Punching an internal extension, she said, "Steph? Can you come in here a minute?"

Her hail was answered immediately by her clinical coordinator—a pretty redhead with freckles galore and enough self-confidence to wear lime green on a regular basis. "Yes?"

Ignoring Nick, who didn't seem in a hurry to go away, Genie tapped a gray folder on her desk. "I just spoke with Richard Sr. and he seemed strange. He wanted to know whether all of his family members had given blood and whether we'd found anything yet."

Steph looked surprised. "We just started that family. And besides, he signed all the releases and I explained them myself. He knows we can't tell him anything confidential."

"Do we have any results from his family yet?"

"No." Steph shook her head and her reddish curls bobbed gently. Genie envied the other woman's curls on a regular basis, though she'd never tell her employee that. "One set of experiments was in the... darkroom yesterday. And the other was set up this morning when the spill happened. I'm going to reexpose yesterday's films and use the developer upstairs, though."

Genie nodded and felt her head swim. She needed to go home. She wanted a nap. "That sounds like a good idea, but you can wait until tomorrow. It's almost quitting time and I think I'm going to head out a little early. You can do the same if you want."

Steph grinned. "Thanks, boss. I've got a date with that cute new rep from Petrie Pharmaceuticals and I wouldn't mind a few more minutes to get ready." She danced an excited little twirl and left in a flurry of red hair and lime green.

Suiting action to words, Genie shrugged on her suede jacket and shut down the computer she hadn't touched all day before she turned her attention to Nick Wellington. He hadn't moved—apparently he shared Dixon's resistance to the words "go away," though she doubted that Wellington felt the same "deep and metaphysical connection to her soul" that George had claimed.

When he followed her to the elevator, she finally had to ask, "What do you think you're doing?"

Wellington shrugged his big shoulders and grinned. Genie's throat tightened and she swallowed hard, trying to force the sudden lightness in her chest to go away. "What does it look like? I'm walking you to your car. Though I'm still not sure you should be driving."

They stepped into the elevator together and when the doors closed, Genie thought that the little space had never felt smaller, even when she'd been stuck for a half hour between floors with two pathologists and a body bag. "The doctor said I'm okay to drive. And you needn't walk me to my car. It's out of your way and I'm okay, honest."

Wellington hit the button for the lobby and the car started down. "Humor me. Sturgeon seems like a good cop, but he and Peters don't seem to have much of a clue who grabbed you yesterday. I'll feel better if I see you home."

The implication wasn't lost on Genie. "You think you're coming home with me?" If she'd been uncomfortably aware of him the night before when she'd been suffering from a concussion, there was no way she'd be any less awkward a day later. "I don't think so. There's no reason whatsoever to think that it was anything other than a random thing. That's what Sturgeon said. Right?"

Wellington held the door for her as they exited onto the street. "Sure, but then there was that spill today... I just don't like it, okay? And is it really so bad to have me around for another night?"

The way he said it sounded so sensible, but Genie was feeling anything but sensible as she and Nick dodged a clump of pedestrian traffic and their bodies bumped together at hip and shoulder. The warm rush of contact sped through her and she knew she was in serious danger of willingly repeating the Archer mistake.

"Can I get your car, Dr. Watson?" With a start, Genie realized they had reached the little Chinatown lot where she had parked her car the day before. The young attendant held up her keys and the late-afternoon sun glinted on them. Parking was at a premium in the city, so lots like this one stacked the cars nose to tail and shuffled them all day long.

She nodded. "Thanks, Randy. I appreciate it."

The diamond stud in Randy's nose winked when he grinned, then sobered. "Are you okay, ma'am? I heard there was some trouble in your lab yesterday."

"She's fine, Randy. Can you just get the car, please? Dr. Watson has a headache and she'd like to go home."

"That was rude," Genie murmured as Randy grumbled off to move the two cars that were blocking in her boring tan sedan. "He's a nice boy."

74   *Dr. Bodyguard*

"And you're dead on your feet." She felt Nick's arm wrap around her shoulders and leaned a little, grateful for the solidity. The warmth. "You need to go home and turn it off for a bit. We'll deal with the rest tomorrow."

Too tired to argue, Genie let her aching head fall to his warm, strong shoulder as they watched Randy shift a blue station wagon out of the way. "Are you always right?" she wondered idly, and she felt him chuckle.

"My ex-wife would say not, and I expect you'll want to deny it tomorrow when you're feeling more like yourself."

"That's right, you were married." Genie didn't want to care, but she had to ask, "What was she like?"

She remembered hearing that the former Mrs. Wellington was blond, beautiful, wealthy—a fit wife for a prince.

"Lucille was...Lucille." Nick might've gone on to say more, but a passing pedestrian bumped Genie from behind and she lost her balance on already shaky legs. She squeaked and clutched at Nick on the way down.

He grabbed a handful of her coat to stop her from falling, and caught her around the waist with his other arm. She swung around and they were suddenly face-to-face, belly to belly. Genie realized she had grabbed handfuls of his shirt to keep upright. She could just feel the scrape of wiry hair beneath her fingertips, the hard, smooth muscle beneath that. The fine tremor that ran through him as he moved—not to push her away this time, but to pull her closer.

The warm lethargy that had stolen through her at the feeling of his arm around her shoulder suddenly bloomed into a tingling burst of heat that burned away the fatigue and the headache and left behind only the feel of the man against her. The sight of his icy blue eyes, darkening as they looked down at her.

Came closer.

Stupid, yelled her brain. *Really, really stupid!*

But she didn't care. She was going to do it and damn the consequences. She stood on shaky tiptoes, closed her eyes, felt his breath on her lips, heard the familiar rattle of her car's engine turning over—

And the world exploded.

Chapter Five

The concussion slapped at Genie with an open fist, driving the air out of her lungs and hurling her into a stinking gutter filled with cabbage and fish left over from the market. She hit hard and gasped, but there was no oxygen in the red-black heat. She sat up and tried to scream.

"Get down, damn it!" She could barely hear the words over a roar that sounded like a hundred T trains coming into Chinatown station at once.

Something pushed her back into the shallow gutter and held her there, and Genie realized there was a thin, rank breath of air among the garbage. She also realized that the great weight pushing her into the filth was Nick, that he was trying to cover her face with his shoulder as the roaring gave way to a strange series of pinging noises as debris rained down around them.

There were screams, running feet, and a second loud explosion that drowned out everything else for a few moments. Genie cowered in the gutter with Nick's arms tight around her as she struggled to understand.

Her car had blown up with Randy inside it.

Someone was trying to kill her.

When the second explosion died down, the banshee wails of a hundred car alarms rose up and Genie and Nick struggled to their feet to see not one but two burning cars. Her boring tan sedan was a black-and-orange inferno feeding off the minivan beside it. The burning cars were ringed by dozens of honking, whooping, wailing automobiles whose flashing head-lights and flickering ambers pointed at Genie as if to say, *You killed him. Randy's dead and it's all your fault.*

"Genie!"

She started to shake as she looked at her car. At the twist of flames that might've been a young man's hand reaching for impossible safety.

"Genie!" She felt Nick shake her roughly and heard him repeat her name again.

"Nick?" The name seemed to pass between lips that belonged to someone else.

"Genie! Are you hurt?" She could tell he was yell-ing, but she could barely hear him over the shrieking cars. She nodded that she was okay, then remembered that he'd asked whether she was hurt, and shook her head no.

"Randy—" she said, then noticed the streak of red running down the back of Nick's forearm and drip-ping off his index finger. "You're hurt."

He turned and tried to get a glimpse of his own shoulder, and Genie realized he'd been hit by some of the shrapnel he'd shielded her from.

"Sit down," she yelled over the sirens, pointing to the curb. He sat, which she counted as a measure of just how much the jagged piece of metal in his shoulder must hurt. She touched the fragment and was appalled to find it burning hot.

She placed her hand on his good shoulder and leaned down to yell in his ear, "We'd better wait for the paramedics."

He didn't look at her, but nodded with his jaw clenched so tightly the muscle balled beneath the skin. He stared out across the street to the lot where the cars still burned and wailed. When Genie stood, she felt Nick's good hand come up to cover hers.

He gripped hard and hung on tight, and together they waited as the car alarms faded and their song was taken up by the sirens of rescuers who were on their way.

But still too late.

"RANDALL BAINES, age eighteen, local address, lives with his mother and younger brother, no father listed." Peters flipped his notebook shut and Sturgeon sucked hard on a peppermint. Genie watched his cheeks move in and out, in and out. It was easier than looking at the smoking husk of her car. Easier than watching the ambulance pull out of the parking lot with its sirens quiet, its lights dim.

There was no hurry for parking attendant Randy Baines. The morgue would wait.

As the charred remains of her car were winched aboard a flatbed truck, Genie's face throbbed and her eyes stung with tears and soot. A crowd had gathered at the small parking area, staring at the devastation with horrified glee. She wondered whether he was out there in the crowd, gloating over his handiwork.

From the way sharp-featured Detective Peters was scanning the mob, she wasn't the only one to have that thought. Not that it would save Randy Baines.

Her eyes stung harder and she didn't even realize she was crying until a hand came out of nowhere and brushed the tears away.

"It wasn't your fault."

She turned to Nick, grateful when he put his good arm around her and pressed her face to his chest, right next to the plain cloth sling the paramedics had insisted on when he refused the E.R.

"It wasn't your fault," he repeated. She could feel his lips in her hair, pressed against her tender scalp, but she found that even Nick couldn't make this pain go away.

"Whose fault was it, then? Randy's? The other people who parked their cars here? Your fault for driving me home yesterday so my car stayed overnight? You're hurt. Randy's dead. Who's fault is it if not mine?"

She pushed away and swayed on her own two feet as they watched the flatbed drive away with what was left of her car. The tow truck paused before pulling into traffic, its brake lights flashing red in the twilight.

Red light. The red of the dark lights in the developer room. Black lights that reflected off of…what? What had she seen? What had she heard? Genie pressed her fingertips to her temples and tried to force her brain to remember. *Behave,* she snapped. *Show it to me! Who did this? Why? How can I make it stop?*

Pain stabbed bright and white behind her eyeballs and she whimpered and sagged, would have fallen to the stinking pavement except for the hand that caught her on the way down.

"That's it. I'm taking you home." Nick half dragged, half carried her to the edge of the crowd and Genie found the energy to resent the fact that even with a heat-cauterized wound the size of a hand on his back, he could still push her around.

"A moment please, Dr. Wellington, Dr. Watson." Sturgeon looked tired and his navy tie with little embroidered fishhooks was wildly askew. Peters, movie-star handsome next to his rumpled partner, stood at Sturgeon's side with his notebook poised and his clever eyes assessing.

"What?" Nick didn't seem inclined to stop to chat with the detectives, but Genie dug in her heels and pulled away. As her headache faded without parting the curtains of memory, she decided she'd rather stand on her own. People around her were getting hurt.

"What's going on? Why is someone trying to kill me?"

Sturgeon nodded and his cheeks puffed in and out, in and out, as another peppermint was reduced to nothingness. In a flash of irrelevancy, Genie wondered whether he sucked them in his sleep.

Behave, she snapped at her brain again. *This is no time for silliness.*

"We'd like to know the same things, Dr. Watson, and we need your help." He turned and gestured toward a drab brown sedan that looked like her ex-car's cousin. "I'd like you to come to the station with us and answer a few questions."

The whole scene was surreal, like something out of

one of her 007 videos or a television cop drama, except that there didn't seem to be any commercial breaks. Genie had the urge to ask if she should call a lawyer, or plead the Fifth, or hold out her wrists for handcuffs.

But instead she walked through the thinning crowd toward the dull brown car, aware of Peters and Sturgeon falling in behind her, Nick following them.

"YOU'RE SURE?" Though he'd already asked her the question twice, Sturgeon still didn't like her answer.

Genie nodded and rubbed her temples, wishing she hadn't turned down the aspirin Nick had offered an hour ago. Wished she hadn't told him to go away, that she'd be fine without him and he should go back to his own life. It would've been nice to know he was waiting for her outside.

"I'm sure. I can't think of a single person I would consider my enemy, certainly nobody who would care enough to hurt me."

"What about George Dixon? You took out a temporary restraining order against him last year," Peters said, referring to a neatly typed page of notes that stood out in stark contrast to his partner's pile of torn notepaper.

Genie shook her aching head. "I know it looks bad, but he's really quite harmless. I took out the order to make a point, not because I was afraid for my life."

Peters glanced at Sturgeon. "We're sure his alibi checks out?"

The older detective shrugged, shuffled a few pages and said, "Seems to. He got coshed in a racquetball game and went to the E.R. for stitches. He's a little less clear as to his exact whereabouts when Dr. Watson was attacked. There's a twenty-minute gap in his logs, but apparently that's not unusual for him. We'll keep working it, though."

Peters turned back to Genie. "Anyone else? Think hard," he suggested, and she resisted the urge to snarl at him that she'd been doing nothing else *but* think hard her entire life, and if she couldn't come up with the name then there probably wasn't one.

"I'm just not the kind of person who inspires strong emotions," she tried to explain. "I can't imagine anyone wanting me dead."

Peters referred to his notes. "But you said that you finished high school by the age of fourteen, college by seventeen and a combined medical degree and a Ph.D. in molecular genetics by twenty-two. Wouldn't that cause some jealousy among your peers?"

Genie laughed. "What peers?" Though she'd outgrown the ache, her defenses were low and she felt tears scratch at the back of her throat. "I was so far outside of the curve that they didn't even grade me. I was a freak, a circus act that the others pointed to and said, 'Wouldn't want to be you!' They didn't hate me. They didn't like me. They didn't really care one way or the other because I wasn't relevant to their lives. I can hardly see how something like that could lead to…"

She couldn't say the word *murder,* it stuck to her tongue like an old peppermint. "Someone trying to hurt me."

Peters looked as though he wanted to argue the point, but Sturgeon stepped in, referring to his own notes. "Then let's focus on the lab since the incidents seem to be centered there."

Genie liked the word *incident.* It was easy and non-threatening and removed the need to say words such as *bomb, rape* and *murder.*

"Okay."

"As of yesterday, we were going under the assumption that your attack was random, not necessarily related to your lab or Dr. Wellington's, but this puts a whole new spin on things. It seems as if you are the target."

"Gee, thanks." Genie's attempt at humor failed before it was born and she dragged a plastic cup of water across Sturgeon's desk and sucked it down, trying to pretend she was chasing four ibuprophen.

If her brain was lying to her, she was damn well going to lie to it.

"What, specifically, does your lab work on, Dr. Watson?"

Yeah, as if she could explain positional cloning in two minutes flat. But she tried. "We're primarily involved right now in what's called 'linkage analysis,' which means using stretches of DNA called 'markers' to follow the inheritance of chromosomes in families that carry a disease."

Both of the detectives had gotten a glazed look in their eyes. She sighed and tried again. "We take families that have, say, Fenton's Ataxia, and look at the twenty-three pairs of chromosomes in each of the family members. If we can find a section of a chromosome that is always identical in family members with the disease and that exact copy is never inherited by people who don't have the disease, then we can say that a gene for Fenton's Ataxia is located on that chromosome. Get it?''

Peters nodded more quickly than Sturgeon, who still looked at her as though she was speaking an obscure dialect of Aramaic.

''Then,'' she continued, ''we narrow the search interval further and further until it's time to look at individual genes and see if we can identify the exact mutation that causes the disease. If we do that, then there's a chance we can cure it, or at least design a better treatment.''

Genie laughed inwardly. It sounded so easy when you put it that way. In reality it could take a lab ten years to find a single disease gene, though the first run completion of the Human Genome Project as well as recent high tech breakthroughs had cut that time down considerably.

Sturgeon nodded with his pen poised over a clean sheet of paper. ''What diseases are you working on right now?''

''Fenton's Ataxia, Gray's Glaucoma and Humboldt's dystrophy are the three biggies. I'm part of international collaborations for Fenton's and Humboldt's, but the Gray's project is all mine. It's a fairly new family that we just enrolled.'' Which made her think of that strange phone call. What was Richard after?

''I'm going to need a list of all your collaborators, as well as your current staff, Dr. Wellington's current staff and your employees going back about five years, particularly anyone you've had to fire or had a bad parting with. Any names come to mind?''

''I'll have Steph put a list together for you.'' Genie's mind raced, selecting and rejecting the people she'd employed since she finished her post doc and started her own lab with the big grant she'd landed on her first application to the National Institute of Health. "As for people I've fired, there have only been a few. I had to let Pansy MacIntyre go because her notes were sloppy and she made bad solutions, but she's five-foot-two and I'm pretty sure she lives in Nebraska with her husband and three kids."

She tried to picture pretty, ineffective Pansy doing something to endanger her manicure, and failed.

"And then there was Derek Joliette. I canceled his post doc when I caught him falsifying results. That's a big no-no. He was pretty angry, and I heard later that he dropped out of the sciences all together because nobody would hire him." The detectives nodded and Sturgeon wrote the name down. "Hey! I don't think he's trying to kill me. You don't have to write his name down!"

Sturgeon continued to write. "Everyone's a suspect until we say otherwise. Anyone else that you fired or fought with in the lab?"

Genie shrugged. "The only two men I've had words with at this institution are George Dixon." She felt a sort of guilty pleasure at seeing George's name underlined in Sturgeon's book. "And Wellington."

"Dr. Nicholas Wellington?"

Genie nodded and felt her face heat. Her whole body flared hot, then cold. "He's not a suspect."

"Everyone's a suspect," Sturgeon repeated. "What did you two fight over?"

She shrugged. "Lab space. Equipment. Personal styles, you name it, we fight about it."

"You seemed pretty cozy in the parking lot," Peters commented, and Genie wondered if this was some lame version of good cop, bad cop.

Or maybe she'd been watching too many police dramas again.

"Yeah, well. I think he feels some sort of misguided responsibility for me since he found me in the darkroom yesterday." She heard her own words and paled even as the detectives perked up.

He found me in the darkroom. Had he known to look there? Perhaps because he had done the deed? Her tired, aching brain reeled with the possibility.

Foolishness. No way. Nick had not attacked her and he certainly hadn't blown up her car. Why would he bother? She was nothing to him.

"Where was Dr. Wellington this morning?"

The parking attendants had moved her sedan several times the previous evening and early that morning as they shuffled cars around the lot. The bomb must have been planted sometime during the day, probably in the late morning when Roach, the other young valet, and Randy had taken an unauthorized break together, leaving the lot unattended for fifteen minutes or so according to a badly shaken Roach.

"In the lab."

"What about before that? We saw him come in just about eleven, when the others were downstairs because of your radioactive spill. Where had he been?"

Genie shook her head, suddenly sore and tired and close to tears. "Errands, I guess. I don't know. He didn't say. You'll have to ask him yourself."

Nick's name went beneath George Dixon's on the suspect list and Sturgeon nodded. "Don't worry. We will."

OUTSIDE THE CHINATOWN police station, Nick stretched his legs, leaned his elbows back on the granite step behind him and took his mind off the burning ache in his shoulder by glaring at the people walking by, trying to figure out if any of them could be *him.* The foot traffic was a mix of commuters and tourists, with the suits on their cell phones galloping past camera-toting visitors who dutifully followed a red stripe painted on the sidewalk.

Nick wondered whether the tourists ever looked up from the Freedom Trail long enough to see the sights that the red line passed near, or whether they just hunted that stripe from end to end and patted themselves on the back when they finished and told their friends back home that they had followed the Freedom Trail while they were in Boston.

A thin, pale, sickly looking man with cornrows in his greasy orange hair and needle tracks on his arms, squirmed and swore as a pair of uniforms wrestled him into the station. After the door shut on the junkie's scrawny behind, Nick watched an expensively clipped poodle urinate on the Metro Police sign while its owner stared off into the distance, whistling.

Nick relaxed a fraction. Genie was safe inside, and when she emerged he was going to be waiting for her whether she liked it or not.

He'd never experienced anything quite as terrifying as the noise and the heat and the stench of that car exploding, and he only thanked the fates she hadn't been in it. It was terrible that a young man *had* been in the car, but it underscored the new truth.

This wasn't random. Someone was after Genie and Nick was darned if he knew why or who. But he knew for sure that whoever it was had just declared war, and that the former opponents in the Battle of the Thirteenth Floor were going to have to join forces to meet their new enemy.

And damn the consequences.

The door to the police station banged open and Nick looked up quickly, half expecting to see the junkie come flying out with an empty handcuff dangling from one wrist. But it wasn't an escaping prisoner. It was Genie.

Something tightened in his chest with an almost audible click, and Nick swallowed hard. She looked weary, almost transparently pale, and her gray eyes practically dominated her face. The bruise on her cheek was a violent purple-black and her stitches looked angry, as though she had frowned so hard she had pulled them apart.

He stood while she descended the stairs slowly, as if each step was an almost inconceivable effort for her tired body. "Genie."

She jerked at the word and whipped her gaze to his. He stepped forward, hands outstretched. "It's me. Nick."

Backpedaling, she caught her heel on the next step up and would have fallen and hit her head on one of the granite pillars that flanked the station doors, but Nick lunged up the stairs to catch her around the waist. She was stiff in his arms. Trembling. And her gray eyes were full of grief and anguish and…fear? Of him?

When she was steady on her feet, Nick took his hands away and held them up. "You're okay. It's okay."

He tried to make his voice soothing when he really wanted to punch something. Hard. What had Sturgeon done to her? "What's wrong?" Stupid question, but, if it were possible, she seemed more upset than she'd been when Sturgeon escorted her into the station. "What did they say to you?"

"Why are you here?" Her voice was brittle, close to cracking, and she flinched when the door opened right behind her and a trio of laughing women in bustiers and short skirts brushed her aside to make their way down the stairs.

"Genie, let's go somewhere." Nick held out a hand, willing her to take it. She looked as though she needed a friend. Badly.

The girl at the back of the little group turned and pursed her lips in his direction. "Honey," she said to Genie, "you got a man like this wantin' to go somewhere, you take that hand and go." She winked at Nick and blew him a kiss. "I would."

Great, just what he needed. Help from a Combat Zone working girl.

He sighed when Genie made no move in his direction. "Come on, let's sit down out of the doorway, at least."

She complied, sitting tensely, as if ready to bolt at any moment. "Why are you here? I told you to go home."

Nick grinned and leaned back on the stairs again,

trying to seem relaxed and nonthreatening when he was seething inside. He could picture his little sister Shelly sitting on the mansion steps in a similar pose, telling him to run before the Senator got home.

But Genie's attacker wasn't the Senator, and Genie was absolutely not his sister. And Nick wasn't leaving this time.

"I didn't listen to you. Big surprise, huh?" He forced a chuckle, but she didn't smile back. He sighed. "I was worried about you and I didn't want you to deal with this alone. I would've come inside, but Peters wouldn't let me."

She didn't question that as he might have expected. Instead she asked, "Where were you this morning after you left my house?"

"Where was I? I told you, I had a few things—" Comprehension splashed through his gut like ice water. "I did a couple of errands, then I came in to work. Does that make me a suspect? Did Sturgeon tell you to ask that or did you just come up with it on your own? What the hell is with that? I've got a hole in my shoulder from a bolt that had your name on it, and suddenly I'm the bad guy?"

He rose and towered over her, cursing himself as she shrank back against the stonework. "I'm not going to hit you for chrissake. I don't hit women." He kicked one of the stone pillars as past and present got jumbled up in his mind and the whole mess shot through with a heavy jolt of disappointment that she thought so little of him. "Not even aggravating ones. And I sure as hell don't blow up their cars."

He swore again as his anger rose and he gave the pillar another kick as pain sang up his leg. Then he noticed that they were attracting attention. More specifically, *he* was attracting attention. Even the tourists had looked up from the red-painted line to watch the scene on the stairs. He could see the headlines now: Senator's Son Arrested For Domestic Violence At The Entrance To Chinatown Police Station. Great.

He forced the anger down to a simmer, turned toward the street and gave a piercing, two-fingered whistle like the gardener in Monterrey had taught him to do when he was ten. A yellow cab screeched to a halt at the curb, almost crushing a pedestrian who gave the cabbie an irate finger before continuing his cell phone conversation.

"Get in." Nick hustled Genie into the cab and shut the door before she could protest. He pulled out his wallet and wrote the taxi number on a scrap of paper.

He leaned in the open passenger side window, rattled off Genie's suburban address and handed the driver a hundred dollar bill. "Get her home and walk her to the front door. Wait while she lets herself in and makes sure everything's okay. If anything looks wrong, call the police right away and mention Detective Sturgeon from Chinatown, then get her the hell out of there. Got it?"

The cabbie grinned at the C-note and nodded. "Got it."

"And I've got your number. Anything happens to her and you're dead, got it?"

Again the nod, this time without the grin. "Got it."

Genie spluttered, "What do you think you're—"

"Don't bother," Nick snarled. "Your car blew up, remember? The last commuter train left an hour ago. I was waiting around to take you home, but I don't think that's such a good idea anymore. You might decide I'm going to drive you out to the reservoir and leave you there under a pile of leaves. So I'll send you home instead and call Sturgeon to have someone look in on you.''

He leaned farther into the cab and wasn't proud when she squished herself against the back seat. ''I stuck around last night because you looked like you could use a friend. I'm not feeling so friendly just now, so I think you'd better go.''

He yanked his head out of the window, slapped the top of the taxi and snapped, ''Drive.''

The cabbie drove, and the last thing Nick saw of Dr. Eugenie Watson was a pair of wounded gray eyes and a narrow, white hand pressed against the taxi window.

FOOL! SHE WAS SUCH A FOOL. What had she been thinking?

Genie knew the answer to that. She hadn't been thinking at all. She had reacted like a cornered animal. Unsure of where the real danger was coming from, she had lashed out at the first thing that moved before deciding whether it was friend or foe.

It was a friend. Or at least it had been.

Safe in her condo with Galore playing in her lap and Oddjob stretched across the headrest of the over-stuffed chair, Genie could admit she had been wrong. She'd let Peters and Sturgeon influence her when in her heart she knew darned well that Wellington wouldn't hurt her.

Her heart? No, no. That was wrong. She knew it

in her head, not her heart. Her brain was capable, predictable. Logical. It didn't make mistakes.

Hearts made mistakes.

Well, sugah, sometimes your heart knows better than your head anyway. For an instant, hearing Marilynn's voice in her mind, Genie could almost feel her college roommate's touch on her hand. It was a firm touch. The touch of strong pianist's fingers. Untrembling fingers.

Marilynn had been Genie's best friend. Her only friend for a while; the sole person on campus who'd seen beyond the IQ to the lonely child beneath and had understood that Genie had needed a mother as much as a friend. Her remembered touch soothed Genie and she looked into both her mind and heart and knew it was no mistake.

Nick Wellington hadn't attacked her. He hadn't ruined her experiments or blown up her car. He had saved her, protected her. And she could swear he'd almost kissed her. Genie remembered the feel of his chest against her fingertips, the hot flush that had climbed her body when they had been nose to nose in the parking lot—before her car had exploded and all hell had broken loose.

"But I was probably just imagining it," she told the cats. "He was just paying attention to me because, I 'looked like I needed a friend.' Well, the heck with him. I've got plenty of friends." She looked down at her lap and thought, Yeah, friends with fur and tails. I've really got to work on that.

She sighed and glanced at the phone. She should call him and apologize. He lived nearby. She could get the number from information, dial it and apologize. Tell him that she was sorry for letting Sturgeon's questions confuse her.

Tell him she wanted to be more than friends.

Where had that come from? But even as her face heated with a fierce blush, Genie's tingling fingers tapped in four-one-one and she requested the number for Nicholas Wellington.

"I'm sorry, ma'am. That number is unlisted."

Darn, darn, darn. Then she thought of calling Steph or Molly to ask if they knew the number, since Genie's techs often went out on Friday nights with the members of the Wellington lab.

Yeah, she could just imagine calling one of her employees and asking for Beef Wellington's phone number. How very high school, or at least the way Genie had always pictured high school. She'd spent those two years alone in a small room where she did individual projects while the other kids labored to learn stuff she'd mastered before the age of five.

Who was she kidding? She was a freak. An over-intelligent child pretending to be an adult. She wasn't a princess fit for the likes of Nick Wellington. She was Genius Watson and there wasn't a darned thing she could do about it.

But that didn't stop her heart from pounding when the phone rang. Oddjob arched his back and hissed.

The phone rang again and Genie glanced at the clock. It was past ten, too late for one of her mother's infrequent calls. It must be Wellington, phoning to yell at her again. *Please, let it be him.* She lifted the receiver and felt her palms sweat.

"N-Nick?"

There was silence on the other end of the line.

"Nick, I was an idiot tonight. I'm sorry. Forgive me?"

Silence.

Then a rasping chuckle that she didn't consciously recognize, one that zapped shivers up and down her spine. "Forgive you? Perhaps I'll forgive you. Maybe I'll even let you live."

The voice was harsh, the breathing heavy, and Genie clutched at the receiver as she saw a flash of black-red light and felt hot breath on the back of her neck, insistent pressure against her buttocks.

"Who...who are you? What do you want? Why are you doing this to me?" Genie knew her voice was rising hysterically but she didn't care. She wanted to know why the monster had chosen her.

Another chuckle, another puff of breath, another involuntary shiver. "This is your second warning, Dr. Watson. Your last warning. Give up the Fenton project or die."

Chapter Six

It was almost midnight when Nick cursed himself as ten types of fool, rolled across the rumpled bedclothes to the phone on the nightstand and punched in the number he had memorized earlier that evening when he'd dialed it five times and hung up each time before it could connect.

It rang once, twice, then was picked up.

"Hello?" The male voice was deep and vaguely familiar. Nick felt a surge of white-hot anger that was as fierce and overwhelming as it was unexpected. How dare she have another man over. It was Nick's job to protect her, not anyone else's.

"Hello?" The voice was annoyed, demanding an answer. "Is anyone there? Hello?"

But Nick wasn't protecting her. He was sulking at home because she had asked a perfectly reasonable, perfectly rational question and he had been insulted by it. In high dudgeon, he had sent her home alone.

She wasn't alone anymore.

Nick heard breathing on the other end of the line. Heavy breathing. A chill raced through him. What if it was her attacker on the phone? What if he'd broken into her condo to finish the job? What if he had raped her? Murdered her.

Clutching the receiver so tightly he heard the plastic creak, Nick said, "If you've hurt one hair on her head, you bastard, I'm going to kill you myself. That's a promise."

Silence. Breathing.

"Did you hear me, you sick son of a bitch? If you've touched her, if you've harmed her in any way, there's going to be hell to pay. Got it?"

A dry chuckle. "I've got it, Dr. Wellington. Very enlightening."

"Sturgeon?" Nick felt a flash of embarrassment, then a new clutch of fear tore at his belly. The fiend had already come and gone. Why else would the police be at her place? "What happened? Is she okay? Is Genie hurt?"

You stupid idiot, you left her unprotected not twelve hours after someone firebombs her car. What kind of a man are you? Not a very good one, Nick assured the Senator. He'd let his own sense of injury put her in danger. He'd never forgive himself if she'd been hurt.

"Dr. Watson is fine. But I think you should come over and stay with her. She's a bit shaken up."

"Why? What happened?"

"He called here just after ten o'clock."

Nick slammed the phone back into its cradle and yanked on his jeans with an oath. He was jamming his head through the armhole of yesterday's T-shirt on the way out the door when a thought struck him.

Lucille would've called him before she called the police, if only to tell him it was all his fault.

"YOUR BOYFRIEND IS on his way over."

The *B*-word brought an illogical rush of pleasure, though Genie felt honor bound to clear up Sturgeon's misconception. "He's not my boyfriend. I just refuse to believe he has anything to do with this, okay?"

The detective's shrug was eloquent, his tone business-like as he ran her through the phone call for the tenth time. She tried to concentrate on his questions while her mind swung between excitement that Nick was on his way and apprehension that he might still be mad.

She'd just about given up on fear, terror and jumping at shadows. It was hard to be too worried when there were two uniforms sitting outside in a cruiser, a rumpled detective drinking coffee at the breakfast bar and a collection of technicians huddled over her phone.

There was safety in numbers.

Then Nick arrived, and it was as if the others didn't exist. His eyes sought hers the second he came in the door, and their ice-blue snapped with temper. Genie fought a sigh. He was still angry.

"Nick—" she began.

"Shut up." He leaned over the couch where she sat clutching her grandmother's quilt to her chest like a shield. "Are you okay?" When she didn't reply right away, he brushed a lock of hair from her forehead and repeated, "Are you okay? Are you hurt?"

"No, I'm—"

"Shut up," he said again, and he kissed her. Hard.

It wasn't a romantic kiss, or a lover's kiss, or a friend's kiss. It was, in its own way, an attack. A statement. A declaration of war, though she wasn't sure anymore which side either of them was on.

She would have protested, would have pushed him away—or pulled him closer, she wasn't sure which—but she didn't get a chance to. While she was still paralyzed with shock, while her brain was still trying to grapple with the fact that Nick Wellington—*Beef* Wellington—was kissing her, it was over.

He pushed himself away and stood, looking down at her with something incomprehensible churning in his eyes. "I'm going crazy," he said to nobody, and stalked into the kitchen.

Genie sat numbly on the couch and vibrated. Too much coffee, she thought, having lost count of the number of cups she'd consumed since the phone call. But the energy that zipped through her was brighter than a caffeine buzz, jazzier than sheer nerves.

Too much tension. She had every right to be stressed, given what she'd been through in the past forty-eight hours. But the liquid fire that raced through her veins and heated her insides was hotter than fear, stronger than terror.

I'm afraid, she thought, and she was. She didn't know who was doing this, didn't know why. Didn't know how to stop him. But the trembling in her thighs wasn't the same as the bone-deep chill she'd gotten from her caller's raspy voice and dead inflection.

It was Nick. She glanced toward the breakfast bar and intercepted Sturgeon's lifted eyebrow. *Not your boyfriend, huh?*

Genie scowled back, then glanced at Wellington. He was wearing the same T-shirt he'd had on at the lab, but his hair was appealingly mussed and his socks were missing. He'd been in bed.

The image that brought to mind was one of warm pink flesh and tangled sheets. Of damp, musky sighs and gentle, sliding touches. Of flash and flame.

Her cheeks heated and Nick's eyes looked straight into hers. His nostrils flared and ice-blue melted to boil in an instant, as if he knew exactly what she had been thinking. As if he was thinking it, too. Genie slammed her eyes down into her lap and concentrated on her own tangled fingers while her lips tingled at the memory of his touching them.

He had an ex-wife as blond and beautiful and tall as Genie was dull and ordinary and short. If the princess hadn't been enough for him, then who was Genie to try?

Madness. Insanity. She was falling for Nicholas Wellington, a man so far out of her league that the only reason they were in the same room was because of a murder and a phone call. A man who ordinarily wouldn't even speak to her in the elevator except to complain about her use of the spectrophotometer.

A man like Archer who could have any woman he ever wanted and would therefore never need a freak like Genius Watson.

"Genie?" It was Nick's voice.

She looked up. "Yes?" The technicians had gone, presumably leaving gadgetry on the phone that had carried that raspy, horrible voice to her.

"The detective is going to need a list of all the people involved in the Fenton's Ataxia project, all the other labs and their people, and the names of the enrolled families."

Genie glanced at Nick, then Sturgeon. "I can't do that."

"What? Why not?"

"I can tell you the names of all the researchers, that's not a problem." She gestured helplessly. "But I can't tell you the names of the study enrollees. It's unethical."

Sturgeon twitched as if the word gave him a rash. "Why? It's not like you're a priest or a psychologist."

"True, but there are huge confidentiality issues in genetic research. There is no disclosure of study volunteers, period." She shrugged helplessly. "I know he said this is about the Fenton's project, but I can't do it. I can't tell you who's in the study."

And she probably wouldn't have even if it had been possible. The search for the Fenton's Ataxia gene was too dear to her, too important. She closed her eyes for a moment and remembered a beloved voice, pictured a pianist's hands turned to claws by the relentless, deadly disease.

Fenton's Ataxia, with its progressive tremors, neurodegeneration, and drawn-out, painful death had taken Marilyn. For that, she had vowed to see the disease cured.

Nick chuffed out a breath. "Even if it's your life we're talking about?"

"I know what we're talking about, Wellington, I'm not an idiot. But I don't see what the families have to do with it. Each person signs a release before blood is drawn, then they have several weeks to back out of the study before their DNA is processed." She sighed. "I can't imagine a family member wanting to stop the project."

"Who might?"

Nick answered Sturgeon's question. "How about the pharmaceutical company holding patents on the drugs that are currently used to treat Fenton's? It's a common enough disease that there's big money in treating it. Discovery of a gene could either update the treatment or suggest a cure, so the company might be looking to stall completion of the project."

Genie was skeptical. "Oh, come on, that's something out of the movies. Real people don't hurt each other over things like that."

Both men looked at her as if she were, in fact, an idiot. Sturgeon said diplomatically, "You'd be amazed at the things people do for money, Dr. Watson. I've seen worse done for far less." He wrote something down on a scrap of paper. "How can I find out who holds those patents?"

"I'll do it." Nick sat on the couch next to Genie, his thigh brushing against her lower back where she curled on the far cushion. She couldn't decide whether to slide closer or to scoot away. "I've got a friend in the P.T.O.—the Patent and Trade Office. I can find out what company's holding the Fenton's patents and whether they've got anything big coming down the pipeline."

Of course he had a friend. People like Nick had friends all over the place. She was probably gorgeous, too, and popular. Genie scowled and pushed away from him on the couch.

Sturgeon nodded. "That'd be good. Also put together a list of any other labs working on Fenton's that might be in competition with this group. They might be trying to shave the odds a little in their favor.''

Genie closed her eyes. They were talking about *scientists* here. Researchers. People who dedicated their lives to understanding human disease. Not thieves. Not gangsters or drug dealers or…mad bombers.

"This is all wrong," she murmured.

Nick patted her thigh, then pulled his hand away as if he hadn't intended to touch her. "I know, Genie. It's weird thinking about scientists being capable of violence, isn't it? But money can be a powerful motivator."

He understood her too easily. Genie wasn't used to being understood. She was used to thinking far more quickly than the people around her, often leaping to conclusions while they were still working through how to ask the question. Nick was so fast he was almost ahead of her.

She wasn't sure she liked it.

"I still don't think it has anything to do with the lab," she insisted.

"Then what? Are you involved in some other Fenton's project? Do you manufacture sports equipment in your spare time? Do you sell popcorn to movie theaters?" Nick referred to several other popular Fenton brand names and Genie wanted to smack him between the eyes for mocking her.

"No. I just think you two have it all wrong."

"Then what do you think is going on, Watson? You're the smartest person in this room, yet I haven't heard a single theory out of that pretty mouth of yours." Nick poked her and she moved further away on the couch until she was crammed up against the armrest. "Who do you think is doing this?"

"I don't know!" she yelled, and was gratified to see both men flinch at the volume. "Don't you get it? I don't have the faintest idea what happened in that darkroom. I don't remember who did it, and because I don't, there's a boy lying in the morgue tonight who didn't need to be there. Okay? You get it? I don't know."

Without a word Nick leaned over and pulled her into his lap. Genie froze in shock, half expecting him to shake her for being such a bitch. But he didn't. He pressed her face against his shoulder and wrapped both arms around her, rocking slightly. "Shh. It's okay. Never mind that now, okay?"

She should have been insulted at his treatment, should have felt foolish being rocked like a child— or as she imagined most children must be. Her own parents had been unsure how to deal with a prodigy. They'd been mystified that they had produced such a strange little girl, and though they had tried to love her, Genie had long ago realized they had been a bit afraid of her, too.

She supposed it had been hard to cuddle a five-year-old who could do differential equations in her head while reciting Proust.

Nick had no such worries. He must've sent Sturgeon some sort of secret male signal over her head, because the detective muttered something about talking to them later that day, said that a squad car would make regular runs past the house, and left. Genie kept her eyes closed. She'd complain about Nick's high-handed tactics in a moment. Right now she was too comfortable to move.

His heart beat steadily beneath her unbruised cheek and at each breath he took, she rose and fell a little, too, finally realizing that they were breathing in tandem.

"I'm sorry, Genie."

She frowned when he spoke, having been perfectly content to sit in silence for a year or so. She sighed. "I'm sorry, too. I shouldn't have asked you where you were this morning. I never really believed what they were saying, but I think I went crazy for a few minutes there in the police station."

"It was a reasonable question. I'm just sorry I didn't handle it better. I should have been here for you when he called. My fault."

She shook her head. "I'm not your responsibility, Nick. I'm grateful that you found me in the darkroom, that you stayed with me last night, and I'm really, really grateful you shoved me into that gutter, but I'm a big girl. You needn't feel like you have to take care of me. I'll be okay. Honest."

Nick pushed her head back down to his chest with a rumbling chuckle and said, "Don't worry about it now, sweetheart. Go to sleep. We'll figure it out in the morning."

But suddenly she wasn't sleepy. She was energized. Twitchy. Ready for action.

She lay as still as she could, hyperaware of the man beneath her, of his breath against her cheek, of the softness of his T-shirt against her neck and hands. Of the way his legs pressed against the backs of her thighs and the fact that her robe had fallen aside so her bare calf was rubbing against the rough denim of his jeans.

Sighing, she snuggled closer, sliding her cheek back and forth against his chest and burrowing into him until she was warm from the inside out.

And growing rapidly warmer.

She shifted again, just for the sheer sensual pleasure of it, and wiggled a little deeper into his lap.

"If you're not sleepy, why don't we watch a movie?" In a single move, Nick slid her off his lap and stood, jamming his hands into his jeans' pockets as if his life depended on it. "You have any videos?"

He stalked to the entertainment center on stiff legs and Genie repressed a sigh of disappointment. He wanted to watch a movie. Obviously he wasn't feeling the same things she was.

Again, big surprise.

"Bottom door, left-hand side." Her face, which moments before had been warm from rubbing against the springy chest hair she could feel through the worn T-shirt, heated again when he glanced at her videos and let out a low whistle.

"You've got quite a collection here."

She squirmed and tugged the robe down over her legs. "Don't tell anyone, please."

That got his attention. He turned in the act of loading a movie into the VCR. "Don't tell anyone what?"

"What kind of movies I watch." Genie gestured surrender. "It's a vice."

Chuckling, Nick shoved the cassette the rest of the way into the machine and fast-forwarded through the opening garbage. Once the FBI warning was on the screen he returned to the couch, slung a friendly arm across Genie's shoulders and tugged until she was leaning against him as the opening chase unfolded.

"Sweetheart," he whispered in her ear, making little shivers run down her neck and coalesce in her belly. "Where I come from, James Bond isn't a vice." They watched 007 jump a motorbike off a cliff and freefall until he caught up with the airplane that had gone over the side just ahead of him.

Nick sighed with heartfelt appreciation when the deep, twanging notes of the theme sounded. "It's a religion."

THEY WATCHED *GOLDENEYE* and debated the merits of the BMW Z3 versus Bond's trademark Aston Martin. They watched *A View to a Kill* and argued Roger Moore versus Sean Connery, but it wasn't much of a debate. They watched *Goldfinger* as their eyelids grew heavy and the dawn's early, bloody light crawled across the sky as a dark sedan rolled to a halt outside the house.

A window slid down and a camera lens was extended, flashing twice, three times, on the license plate of Nick's Bronco before the sedan rolled away, unremarked by the officer dozing in his car.

Chapter Seven

"Rough night, boss?" Jared shot a tattooed elbow into Nick's ribs and chuckled. "You look a little fuzzy around the edges."

Nick stared at the ninety-six well plate on the lab bench. He was pretty sure he was supposed to measure a minute quantity of something and put it in each of the small wells, but he'd be darned if he remembered what it was or why he was doing it.

He'd also be darned if he'd ask Jared.

While taking a surreptitious look at his own lab notebook in case it had a clue, Nick answered, "Yeah, you could say that. We sort of forgot to go to sleep."

Jared whistled and pulled his baseball cap lower over his brow. "You go, boss. Hooked yourself a real wildcat this time, did you? Does she have a sister?"

Aha. Nick read a few sentences in his own handwriting and blessed the grad school advisor who used to fine him beers when he forgot to write stuff down. Fluorescent sequencing. He was supposed to be rerunning those last fifty base pairs for the article he was putting together. He could do that. Piece of cake. He grinned and got to work.

"Or are you saving the sister for yourself? Come on, come on, fess up. Tell Uncle Jared everything."

There was a muffled question from three benches over, where Jill was walking a grad student through the steps of DNA purification, and Jared answered with a loud, "The boss had a hot date last night and he didn't get a wink of sleep, poor baby. She was an animal."

Jared flickered his studded tongue grotesquely and Nick's fatigue fuzzed brain finally got a grip on the conversation. "Hey, wait! It wasn't like that. We just talked!" And watched movies and ate popcorn and sat next to each other on the couch with a pair of cats named after the bad guys in *Goldfinger*.

And had so much fun they forgot to go to sleep, even though the specter of a faceless killer had hung over the overstuffed couch and lurked in the shadows beyond the kitchen, waiting for them to let down their guard. Nick's only consolation was that she'd let him drive her to work that morning and that she was safe in her office now, working on her own neglected experiments while the detectives did their jobs.

"Sure, boss. If you say so." Jared winked and shot another pointy elbow into Nick's ribs.

Sighing, Nick rubbed at his chest and wished his staff was as disciplined as Genie's. Maybe if he wore a suit and tie to work every day they would give him more respect.

Yeah, as if that was going to happen in a million years.

"So, does she have a sister you could hook me up with?"

Jill finally came to Nick's rescue, hustling over from her bench and grabbing Jared by an earring. "Can't you see the man is busy? Let him alone and get back to your own work. If you can't concentrate on that, then you can go help maintenance bleach the developer room." The idea obviously appealed. She grinned and said, "In fact, you can go down the hall and grab a brush right now. Make sure every trace of…well, you know, is off the walls and sink before poor Dr. Watson has to go back in there, got it?" She sent him off with a kick in the rear. Surprisingly, he went.

Jill could get away with stuff like that because everyone loved her.

"You just talked, huh?" She folded her arms across her pristine lab coat and leaned back against the high bench. "All night?"

Nick sighed again and wished he could lock his office door and take a nap, preferably with Genie right next to him so he could be sure she was safe. "Doesn't anyone have anything better to worry about this morning? Has it escaped your attention that there's a madman running around, attacking women and blowing up cars? Doesn't that worry any of you?"

"Of course it does, Nick. We're all worried about Dr. Watson. But we're also your friends." She glanced in Jared's direction. "Or at least I am. And I'm worried about you, too. In all the time I've worked for you, I've never seen you this way."

"What way? Oh, never mind." Nick stabbed a load

of amplification solution into the sequencing mix and handed the plate to Jill. "Finish this for me, will you? I have to call the detectives."

He snapped off his sterile gloves and tossed them into the trash. Jill handed the plate to her nervous-looking grad student and Nick stifled a groan. If he hadn't fouled up the chemical mix himself, the student was sure to mess up the programming. He could kiss that sequencing goodbye.

"And Jill?"

She turned. "Yeah, Nick?"

"Try to keep Jared quiet, okay? I don't want it spreading around that I'm having fun while there's a madman stalking Dr. Watson. It just doesn't seem appropriate, you know?"

Jill nodded and flashed a quick smile. "I'll see what I can do, but it's going to be a little difficult to control the rumors."

Yawning hugely, Nick asked, "Why's that?"

"Dr. Watson is in her office, fast asleep on her light box." Jill shrugged and grinned. "Rumor has it she had a late night, too. Go figure."

Nick laughed and opened the door to his office. The poster of the Face of Erectile Dysfunction grinned at him and he shook his head as he closed the door.

GENIE FROWNED AT THE little black bars when they swayed, merging and separating before her very eyes like tiny line dancers. "Stay still, darn it."

Or maybe it wasn't the shadows on the X-ray film that were moving. Maybe it was her head, bobbing around on her neck again as it had just before she fell asleep on her desk. But the light box, a white plastic rectangle lit from the inside for use as a horizontal X-ray viewer, was so warm and smooth. It was begging her to sleep on it again.

How humiliating. Dr. Genius Watson, sleeping on the job.

But it had been worth it. She couldn't remember another night that she'd had so much fun, even though the circumstances were less than ideal. In fact, they downright sucked. But that hadn't stopped her and Nick from snuggling on the couch until the wee hours of the morning. Who needed sleep? She had Wellington.

Whoa, there. She frowned. *You don't have Nick. He's just being a nice guy, keeping you company while the police figure out what's going on. He's a white knight at heart. It's nothing personal.*

Nothing personal. Like it had been "nothing personal" when handsome, golden boy Archer had roughly relieved her of her virginity and then told her that half of his fraternity was waiting outside in the hall for her to emerge and prove that he, Archer Cavanaugh, had screwed the inscrutable Genius Watson. He had really done her a favor, he insisted, because she could no longer be voted The Most Likely to Die a Virgin.

Maybe not. But virgin or not, she decided she'd die before she walked through that door, so when Archer had left the room to accept back-slapping congratulations, she'd gone out the window and down the three story rose trellis. In an ice storm. And had gone straight to Marilynn, who had probably saved her life that night.

And while she'd survived, and the gossip was

quickly replaced with the news of Marilynn's illness, the lesson had stayed with Genie as surely as any other she'd learned in college.

No more rich boys. No more mistakes.

And Genie knew that when she let her heart lead the way, she made mistakes. When her brain was in control, she was in control. It was as simple as that. She had to stay in control, and that was more important now than ever before.

There was someone out there who didn't want the Fenton's project to move forward, and there was a man in the office down the hall who was nothing more to her than a gentleman. Maybe a friend. Never a lover.

Okay, then, brain. Let's get back to work. No more arguments from you, hear?

She frowned down at the film again, then picked up the pedigree of Richard's family.

She scanned the pedigree, which was a chart of the people, their relatedness, affected status and other pertinent information. She thought briefly of Richard's strange phone call—and shoved aside thoughts of another, less benign voice on the phone—as she compared the information on the pedigree to the data on the X-ray film. She frowned.

Something wasn't right.

She traced her finger down the lanes on the film. Her trained eye could pick up each of the two copies an individual inherited—one from the mother, one from the father. But one of the lanes, marked FNTN-III.7, was aberrant. This person inherited a marker from his mother, but his second copy didn't match either of his father's.

Too tired to hike down the hall, Genie called the lab extension from her office phone and was pleased when it was answered with a professional, "Good morning, Watson lab. How may I help you?"

"Good morning, Terry. How did those Humboldt's amplifications come out yesterday?"

Terry swallowed audibly and she pictured his prominent Adam's apple bobbing up and down. In the fifth year of his graduate studies, Terry would graduate in another year with a truly outstanding thesis that had grown out of the Humboldt's project. He was awkward, brilliant, and Genie suspected he had a mild crush on her.

"F-fine, Dr. Watson. Should I bring the results to your office?"

"No, not right now. How about after lunch? Right now I need to see Steph in my office. Can you ask her to join me?"

Genie replaced the receiver with a smile. Terry reminded her so very much of herself. Overbright, overeducated and socially awkward around people he might find attractive. But Terry had one advantage she had lacked. His physicist parents had been fully capable of dealing with a child prodigy.

On the other hand, Genie's mother Vivien, a French fashion designer who had fallen in love with an American financier, had been happy to give her daughter into the care of a succession of special schools. Vivien had had better luck with her younger son, Etienne, who had moved with her to Paris after her husband's death in a small commuter plane crash. Etienne was handsome, outgoing and of dead-average intelligence.

Genie had often thought that she could walk past her mother and brother in a crowd and not even recognize them. She still missed her father from time to time, though. He had been the one to visit her at school and call her when she was ill. Upon his death, Genie had been the beneficiary of a large life insurance policy and half his estate, as if her father knew he hadn't given her a good family and was trying to make up for it with money.

"Dr. Watson? You wanted to see me?" Steph's red curls bobbed gently in the doorway and she looked concerned. "Is everything okay? Are you okay? Do you need anything?"

Genie felt a small glow of warmth and had the sudden urge to hug her entire staff. Two days earlier she would have sworn that not one person working in the Watson lab would notice if she just disappeared one day. They worked for her, they respected her, but Genie hadn't thought they liked her very much.

How wrong she had been. When she'd come into her office that morning her desk had been covered with flowers, cards and even a stuffed teddy bear wearing a white lab coat, a test tube in its paw.

She didn't think anyone had ever given her a stuffed toy before. She kept it on the top of her bookshelf and grinned at it from time to time with an unfamiliar sense of belonging.

"I'm fine, really. Just a little tired." Genie smiled at Steph's concern, feeling that warm flicker again. She'd hired Steph two years earlier, drawn by the look of quiet desperation in the back of the young woman's eyes, coupled with impeccable references from an unfinished graduate degree. The single mother of a tiny girl, Steph had relaxed over time and had even begun to smile again in the past few weeks. Genie wondered whether the change had anything to do with the girl's new beau, Roger.

Genie was beginning to understand the feeling.

She flipped the pedigree to face the other woman. "I wanted to ask you about the new family. See this guy, III.7? On the two films I've read so far, he's an outlier. Either we have a DNA problem or the pedigree's wrong. Can you get his file from down the street and check the DNA stocks to make sure he's labeled correctly?" She thought of Richard's promised donation to the Eye Center and tapped the film. "We can't afford any question marks on this family, if you know what I mean."

Steph frowned. "I don't think I met that patient in person. Darlene enrolled him. She was helping because it had gotten so crazy. It was a super busy day, so we might have mixed up a sample. I tried to be extra careful, though."

"I'm sure you were," Genie assured her. "I'm not looking to place blame, I'd just like to figure this out before we go much farther with the project."

"Of course." Steph wrote the identifying code on a piece of paper. "I'll call over to the Eye Center and get the original files. How about extracting his second pellet?"

Each study volunteer gave three tubes of blood that were turned into DNA pellets. If the mix-up had occurred during that part of the experiment, the pellet marked FNTN-III.7 actually could belong to a different member of the family, which would account for him sharing some of the correct DNA but not all of it.

Genie nodded. "Good idea."

Clutching the piece of paper in her hand, Steph headed for the door. Not quite ready to face calling Sturgeon, which was the next thing on her to-do list, Genie said, "Steph?"

The redhead turned at the door. "Yes?"

"How was your date yesterday? The one with Roger from Petrie Pharmaceuticals?"

It was probably the first time Genie had ever asked her staff a personal question, but Steph handled it well. She only blinked. "It was— It was okay. We went after, you know, after your car…"

Genie winced. "Sorry about that."

Steph gave a slightly pained grin. "Not exactly your fault, you know? Anyway, he wanted to go see the car, but by the time we got there it'd been taken away. I was glad about that. Then we went out to dinner and he brought me home early. I think he had something to do after, but that was okay since I was pretty wiped out. He's nice. I think this one's a keeper."

How do you know which one is a keeper? How do you know if he likes you at all? Genie wanted to ask, but she couldn't. It would hardly be professional of her.

"I like your hair that way," Steph said, startling her.

Genie touched the springy locks self-consciously. Her stitches and scalp still hurt too much for her to twist the hair up, so it flowed freely down her back. She'd worn one of her brown suits though, as a way of forcing her body to believe that they were actually going to work on zero sleep. "You do?"

Steph nodded. "It looks good that way and it has all sorts of interesting highlights. It makes a nice contrast to the suit, though I have to say that I really liked that sweater you had on yesterday with the jeans." She added slyly, "And so did Dr. Wellington. I saw him checking you out a couple of times."

"You did? He was? I mean—" From a breath of hope to utter, juvenile embarrassment, Genie dropped her head in her hands, wincing as the stitches across her eyebrow pulled. She pictured the sight that had greeted her in the mirror that morning and winced again.

The Frankenstein look. How sexy.

"Never mind," she muttered, then glared at Steph, daring her to laugh.

She didn't. In fact, she didn't seem to find the thought ludicrous at all. "Yeah, he was. We all think it's really cute how he's gotten all studly and protective over you. Who would've thought? You and Beef Wellington." But she still wasn't laughing.

"He's just feeling territorial because of what's happened the last few days, that's all. When Sturgeon and Peters arrest this creep, things'll go back to normal around here. No more protective-stud stuff." Genie's face burned as she said the word stud. It brought to mind all sorts of delicious things.

"Do you want it to go back to normal?"

"Of course I do. I want to be able to work in my own lab again. To go home at night and not worry about creepy calls." Home alone. Without Nick. She squeezed her eyes shut. "No. I don't want it to end then. Okay? But it's going to. He's so far out of my league it's ridiculous, okay? Are you happy now? Go back to work.''

"Hmm. It looks to me like you could use a break from all this.'' Steph gestured down the hall, though Genie wasn't sure whether she meant to point toward the developer room or to Nick's office. Or both.

Instead of leaving Steph reached across Genie's desk, picked up the phone and dialed an extension. "Jill? Finish up what you're doing, get Molly and meet me at the elevators. We have a mission. And bring your passkey because I can't find mine.''

A mission. That sounded like fun. Genie never had missions; she had jobs. Projects.

Steph held out her hand. "Come on, Dr. Watson.''

"Come where?'' Genie allowed herself to be hauled out from behind the desk and propelled toward the door. "Where am I going?''

Steph wrapped an arm around Genie's shoulders and steered her toward the elevators, where Nick's assistant Jill and Genie's tech Molly were already waiting, dressed in their light fall-weight coats. "We're going shopping.''

"Oh.'' Genie stopped just inside the hall, feeling like an outsider when she saw the three grinning friends waiting together by the elevator for a lunchtime excursion. "I'd better let you get going.''

"No, dummy.'' Steph grabbed Genie by the arm and pushed her through the elevator doors as soon as they opened. "*We're* going shopping. To be exact, the three of *us*—'' she indicated herself, Jill and Molly "—are taking *you* shopping. If you're going gunning for game as big as Beef Wellington, you're

going to need some stronger ammunition than that.''
She indicated Genie's sensible brown suit.

The doors closed. Genie was trapped in the descending elevator with a trio of lab techs bent on a makeover.

"But I—I'm not 'gunning' for anyone, certainly not Dr. Wellington.'' She didn't bother to defend her suit. She knew it was boring. Unsexy.

Grown-up.

Molly rolled her eyes. "Then you're blind as well as stupid.'' She then glanced over at her boss and cringed. "I can't believe I just said that.''

Genie didn't think anyone had ever called her stupid before. She kind of liked it. It sounded very normal. However, in this case, she wasn't stupid.

He was way out of her league. They'd even said it themselves: *big game*. But she smiled shyly at Molly. "Consider me neither blind nor stupid.''

The elevator doors opened and the four women joined the lunchtime crowd streaming out of the building. They paused outside the building and Steph, the ringleader, turned to Genie.

"We'll be safe in Chinatown as long as we stick together, okay? So nobody goes anywhere without the others, and if anything happens it's rape-whistle first, pepper-spray second. Agreed?'' When everyone nodded, she linked her arm through Genie's and started walking. "So? Do you like Nick?''

Molly snickered. "What is this, high school?''

"It's a valid question,'' Steph insisted, and Jill nodded.

Genie dug her toe into a chunk of loose mortar as they waited for a light to turn. "He's not... He doesn't…'' She blew out an impatient breath. Now she was starting to *sound* like a dummy. What was happening to her? This is why she stayed away from men. And women. Interpersonal relationships were more complicated than X-ray films. She tried again. ''I don't…''

''She doesn't think he likes her,'' Molly translated.

Jill grinned and said, ''He's crazy about her. You should see him today. He's walking around in a fog, talking to himself and whistling something that sounds like the theme from *Live and Let Die*. Is this the Dr. Wellington we all know and drool over?''

The others shook their heads in the negative and Genie felt a spurt of excitement. He might actually be thinking of her if he was whistling a Bond theme.

Or else he was just delirious from exhaustion.

''But why doesn't he…'' Genie broke off with a groan. ''Never mind.''

''He doesn't…? Oooh.'' Jill grinned. ''Why don't you tell us all about it while we buy you a new wardrobe that'll ensure he…does, if you get my meaning.'' Keeping a sharp eye on the pedestrian traffic, looking for…who knew what, they threaded their way through the garment district that backed up to Chinatown.

''And I need to pick up something for Friday night,'' added Steph.

''Another date with Mr. Petrie Pharmaceuticals? Do tell, Steph! This Roger sounds like the real deal, kiddo. And you deserve it after all that you've been through.'' Jill swung them toward one of the designer markdown basements. ''And then Molly can tell us about Charlie the Wonderlover from Bentley's yeast lab—I personally could never date a man who worked with yeast—and then I'll complain about having to share my lab bench with Jared.''

Genie stalled on the threshold of the store and the others looked at her. Molly asked, "Something wrong?''

"I—'' Genie scrambled furiously to put the feeling into words. This is what friends do, she thought, they go shopping at lunch and talk about their lives. This is what Marilynn and I used to do.

These days she shopped alone or ordered from a catalog when she was busy. It was an errand, a chore to be handled when necessary. It wasn't a pleasure. Wasn't a social event.

Jill's eyes softened and she touched Genie's shoulder. "My brother was a concert pianist by the age of seven. He didn't have many friends when he was a kid. He still has a hard time being around people his own age, but he's learning.''

Genie nodded gratefully. Somebody understood, if only a little. It helped. She took a deep breath and tried to explain. "It's like I took all these classes, learned all these things I'll never need to know, but somewhere along the line they forgot to teach me all this other stuff, like how to have friends and what to do when the man you're interested in doesn't seem interested in you.''

She gestured to encompass the whole conversation. "I can tell you what hormones are released at what stage of sexual excitation, what blood goes where and which pieces of the brain are activated.'' She shrugged. "But I don't have a clue what to do when he looks at me and I start shivering and sweating at the same time and my stomach quivers like I'm going to throw up but I'm not.''

Jill nodded, Molly fanned herself and Steph pretended to swoon. Genie's lips twitched and she demanded, ''When do they teach you that stuff? Fourth grade? Fifth? High school? Was there a course in college I missed?''

Molly laughed, but it wasn't a cruel laugh. She laughed as though she'd thought the same things once or twice. ''There should be a course, or an owner's manual at the very least, but there isn't. Love is one of those things you make up as you go along. You try stuff and it either works or it doesn't and you learn from your mistakes.''

''But I don't want to make any mistakes.'' She didn't want to practice. She wanted Nick.

Steph grinned and slung her arm across Genie's shoulders in a friendly hug. ''Then you ask your girlfriends for advice.''

Genie smiled tentatively. ''I don't think I've had girlfriends before.'' Not for a long time, anyway.

''Well, Dr. Watson, you've got three of 'em now,'' proclaimed Molly, and the others nodded.

Genie felt as if the sun, which had been hidden behind a bank of clouds for so long, had suddenly come out to shine yellow and warm on the little group outside the discount designer store.

''You can call me Genie,'' she said. ''I'm not Dr. Watson. I'm Genie.''

She had friends. A mental note bubbled from the recesses of her brain. *Get a life.*

It seemed she was on her way.

As she and her new friends entered the store, Genie

thought she caught a flash of motion out of the corner of her eye, but when she looked again there was nothing to see. She shrugged.

Must've been a shadow in the sunlight.

WHERE THE HELL WAS SHE? Nick scowled and drummed his fingers on the lab bench. Again. Jared looked up from his experiment, watched Nick fidget impatiently, and looked back down at his notes.

They had repeated this sequence at least twenty times in the past ten minutes.

The lab was quiet. Deserted. Jill had disappeared hours ago, leaving a note that she was shopping and would be back before her experiment was finished running. The new grad student, whose name escaped Nick at the moment, was in class, and Ahmed, the post doc, was off wrangling with officials over his temporary visa. Genie's lab area seemed equally as barren and the whole floor was giving Nick the creeps.

It was as though he and Jared were the only two people left alive on the planet. What a terrifying thought. And the empty labs echoed like the setting for some B-grade horror movie.

Nick's tired mind kept wandering, flickering between trying to figure out where everyone was and picturing an army of animated clown dolls marching through the labs, wreaking havoc on all the equipment and lying in wait for the unsuspecting scientists to return.

Kind of like the guy in the developer room, except he was no clown.

"I've gotta get some sleep," Nick muttered, and

shoved his fingers through his hair in an attempt to rub the fatigue away. "Where the hell is she?"

Then the elevator dinged, the doors opened and there she was. Nick was across the lab and grabbing her arms before he even knew he had moved. "Where have you been? Are you okay? You scared the hell out of me, disappearing like that!"

Genie froze and looked at him like a rabbit pinned in a pair of headlights. "I was…I was shopping. I'm sorry." The fear in the back of her gray eyes leaped to the front. "Did something happen? Was somebody else hurt?" She dropped a trio of shopping bags and grabbed Nick's wrists, which were still on her shoulders. "What happened?" She shook him slightly. "What else happened? Why are you so upset?"

Nothing. Nick inhaled deeply and heard the blood thunder in his ears. Nothing had happened to her. She'd been shopping with the girls. She was fine. Safe. The maniac hadn't gotten her.

But he could have. The adrenaline coursing through Nick's body redirected itself and he grabbed her arms again and shook her slightly, thinking of Lucille, who'd shopped voraciously toward the end of their marriage. "What do you mean, you were shopping? What the hell were you thinking, wandering around the city unprotected when there's a murderer after you?"

The look of fear was replaced by one of pique and she repeated, "I was shopping. And as you can tell, nothing happened to me. We stayed together and we had our rape whistles and pepper spray at the ready. We were as safe—if not safer—than we are here."

She wasn't his problem. She couldn't tell him any

clearer than that. She didn't want or need his help, and that just pissed him off worse. Here he'd been going out of his skull with worry and she was *shopping*. Didn't women ever think of anything else? He bellowed, "He could've grabbed you just now, did you ever think of that? How could you be so stupid?"

That did it. Anger kindled deep in Genie's eyes, flashing silver and red against the clear gray of her irises. She yanked away from Nick and stood facing him with her puny hands balled into fists.

"I've had just about enough of well-meaning people calling me stupid today. Do you hear me?"

In the background Nick saw Jill, Molly and Steph looking on raptly while Jared grinned. The new grad student had come back from class and was trying very hard to disappear behind a notebook.

"Do you hear me?" she repeated. Apparently the question hadn't been rhetorical.

"Uh—"

"Shut up. Do you honestly think that I could forget for one minute what's going on around here? That I could forget a boy was killed yesterday because he turned on my car? That you were hurt? That I was almost raped? Gee, Nick. You must think I'm pretty dumb to forget about all that. Do you think I'm dumb?"

Her anger calmed Nick's to a mellow burn that quickly changed to something else entirely.

He'd never seen Genius Watson like this, with her cheeks fiery red and sparks shooting out of her eyes. She was breathing deep, fast, and her free-flowing hair hissed and crackled around her head as though it too was angry. She glowed from within with a seething, roiling passion borne of anger and frustration and fear, and Nick had never before in his life seen anything so magnificent.

This is how I want her, he thought, *this is how I want her to look beneath me when we make love.*

When. Not if. Somewhere along the last few days, his mild fascination had blossomed to a sizzling lust that blotted out almost every other rational thought save one.

That he could not, *would not,* take advantage of the situation. He would not coax her into his bed when she was in danger, when she was under his protection, vulnerable.

But God help him, he wanted to.

"Well, do you?"

He almost said, *Hell, yes!* until he remembered that the actual question had been whether he thought she was stupid. He didn't think that yes was the answer she was looking for there.

"Uh—"

"Never mind. Of course I'm not stupid. Of course I knew there was danger in me going out today. But do you know what? I'm in danger here in the lab. I'm in danger in my car, or I would be if I still had one, which I don't because the sick son of a bitch blew it up." She muttered, "I've gotta get a new car," as if recording the thought in her brain, then returned to her harangue. "So you tell me, was I really in any more danger going shopping than I am staying right here?"

She included Jared in her question, but he pretended a great and deep interest in a bottle of acetone at his elbow and she turned back to Nick. "Well, do you?"

"No," he said quietly. "I don't think you're any safer here, which is what has me all worked up." He looked straight at her and said, "I care, Genie. Whether you like it or not, whether *I* like it or not, I care what happens to you."

While Genie failed to respond to his declaration, Nick thought he saw the three female techs give each other high fives. The elevator dinged out in the hall and Sturgeon buzzed to be let through the security doors.

Genie hurried to let him in as if grateful for the distraction. "Detective Sturgeon! Did you catch him yet? Are there any new leads?"

Sturgeon returned her greeting absently while his eyes noted who was in the lab.

"Can we go to one of your offices? I have some upsetting news." Sturgeon's cheeks puffed in and out, in and out, in a rapid tempo that bespoke agitation.

Genie balked. "Whatever you have to say you can say in front of my...friends. It seems that they may be in danger just by working here."

"Suit yourselves." Sturgeon pulled out a fresh peppermint and contemplated it. "We found the guy who rigged your car yesterday." He didn't seem overjoyed by the break.

"Where?" Nick had a feeling he wasn't going to like the answer. As if sensing the same thing, Genie moved closer until her arm brushed against his.

"Floating in Boston Harbor with a bullet in his brain."

Chapter Eight

"So you're saying this Ramirez O'Shea was paid to blow up my car?" Genie's stomach roiled and the shrimp tempura she'd giggled over not an hour before threatened a return visit. She was vaguely aware of Nick's solid, comforting presence beside her, but both the happy buzz created by the shopping trip and the heady anger of her temper tantrum had quickly faded in the face of Sturgeon's news.

"That's correct, Dr. Watson. One of our informants reported that Ramirez had come into some serious cash recently, and was overheard bragging that he had been paid to have a little fun at a parking lot in Chinatown."

A little fun. Genie gulped and sternly ordered her lunch to remain where it was. Is that what this was to these people? Fun?

"I'm going to shut down the lab. Now. Today," she blurted. There was no way she was endangering any more lives. If this guy wanted her to close up shop, then she would. He'd done his job and scared her into shutting down.

"Now, don't be hasty," suggested Nick. "You

can't just stop everything in its tracks. Think of your employees. Think of their work.''

''I *am* thinking of my employees. I'm thinking of keeping them alive. That's more important than science, don't you think?''

If someone had told her four days ago that she would value something more than her job, Genie would have snorted and said they were crazy.

''There's no guarantee he'd stop harassing you if you closed the lab, Dr. Watson,'' Sturgeon said. ''Ramirez told our informant that the man who had hired him was, in his reported words, 'not quite right in the head.' Shutting down the lab isn't the answer. Finding this guy is.''

He pulled out a stack of index cards and Genie wondered when her case had graduated from torn notebook paper to index cards. ''Now, I've spoken to all of the primary investigators involved in the Fenton's Ataxia project, and done light checks on most of the employees on the lists you gave me. Nothing has jumped out yet, but we're still looking.''

''How about Dixon?''

Genie turned toward Nick. ''I really think you're wasting your time on George. He's a worm, sure, but worms don't have spines. That applies rather aptly in this case. The only reason I took out that restraining order was to get him to stop singing love songs to my answering machine. He's a nonstarter.''

''My partner would tend to agree.'' Sturgeon paused to unwrap a fresh peppermint, and Genie noticed that today's supply was green-and-white pinwheels. He must've run out of the red ones. ''Detective Peters interviewed Mr. Dixon at his home, confirmed with his doubles partner that the injury came from a racquetball game, and established that Mr. Dixon was playing a fantasy role-playing game at a friend's house at the time of last night's phone call.''

''So he's not a suspect?'' Nick sounded vaguely disappointed and Genie had to sympathize. It would make life at Boston General much easier for the researchers—and the women—if George Dixon went away and took his radiation storm troopers with him.

''Not at this time, although we'll keep checking. He doesn't have a solid alibi for the time of Dr. Watson's attack.''

Attack. In the darkroom. Genie saw a flash of black and red, felt the back of her neck heat with a stranger's breath. She smelled the sharp bite of developer chemicals and heard a harsh voice over the rumble of the machines.

What? What had she seen? What had she heard? Would it give her a clue as to what was going on? Think! She had to think. Had to remember.

She needed to go back into the developer room to see if that jogged the block loose. She had to make her brain behave. Force it to give up the information it was hiding.

''Well, I still don't trust him.'' Nick scowled. ''Not one bit.''

''Have you had a chance to look into pharmaceutical companies with interest in Fenton's Ataxia?'' Sturgeon changed the subject neatly and Genie frowned. She hadn't even thought about calling her salespeople and asking them about Fenton's. She never forgot homework assignments. Never. What was wrong with her?

"I made a few calls this morning." She glanced at Nick, who looked alert and awake, rugged and just mussed enough to make her want to run her fingers through his hair to neaten it. He looked wonderful. And apparently while she'd been sleeping on her lightbox and jumping at shadows, he'd been doing his homework.

"My friend at the patent office unofficially pulled up a few records and told me there are currently three Fenton's patents in the last stages of approval, two of which are suing each other for infringement. All of them are for improvements on the current drugs, not new ones."

"Who owns them?" Sturgeon shuffled to a clean index card, pen poised.

Nick frowned. "Rothman Biometrics, Intelligenetics, and Petrie Pharmaceuticals. They're all fully established companies with good track records."

Sturgeon wrote the names and nodded. "Do either of your labs have contact with these companies?"

"I buy glassware and lab supplies from Petrie." Genie frowned and cudgeled her uncooperative brain. "And I'm pretty sure we bought the automated sequencer and those two centrifuges from Intelligenetics last year. I don't think I've ever done business with Rothman." She turned to Nick. "You?"

He nodded. "I buy from Petrie, too, and we just ordered a half dozen gel boxes from Intelligenetics. Rothman doesn't really sell lab supplies—it's strictly a drug company. I'm not sure there's any connection."

Connections to drug companies. Steph's new boy-friend was from Petrie Pharmaceuticals. Genie shoved the thought away. There was no way she was getting her new friend and her boyfriend into trouble over what had to be nothing more than a coincidence.

No way.

There was a tap at the door. "Dr. Watson? I mean, Genie?" Steph's red head popped around the corner of the door. "I don't mean to interrupt, but the ex-traction on that other pellet is done. Do you want me to rerun that Gray's Glaucoma family with the new DNA?"

Genie remembered the outlier DNA from the morn-ing, the one person that didn't match the rest of his family. Normally such a mystery would excite her and she would spend the next few hours trying out scenarios that would make the data fit. Could he be adopted? The product of an affair? Switched at birth? Or maybe the small section of chromosome they were looking at had an abnormality that could only be seen at the DNA level, a duplication or an inversion that might cause the disease.

But this was no ordinary day and Genie wasn't going to be responsible for anyone else getting hurt. She sighed heavily and shook her head. "I don't think so, Steph. In fact I'm closing up shop for a few days until we get all this sorted out. I want you and Molly to help the others finish up whatever they're working on, freeze it down in the ultralow temps for storage, and take the rest of the week off."

"But I… But we…but." Steph didn't seem as overjoyed at the prospect of a few days off as Genie had expected.

"Consider it a bonus four day weekend. Spend some time with your boyfriend." Genie tried to suppress the flutter of unease. Maybe she should tell Steph about the drug company connection. That was it, she'd give her a quick heads up about the direction Sturgeon's questions were heading, and let Steph decide what to do about it. That way Genie would protect her new friend without siccing the police on her and causing her grief with her new guy.

Mumbling, Steph withdrew. Nick was frowning. "Are you planning on taking the rest of the week off, as well?"

"Of course not." The thought had never occurred to her. "I'm going to stay here and call the other Fenton's labs myself, see if there's anything we're missing. There has to be some reason this person wants the project shut down."

"Unless he's insane and he's fixated on you for no reason," Nick muttered darkly, earning himself a look from Sturgeon.

"That's a possibility you should consider, Dr. Watson, and I also think you should leave town for a few days. Do you have family you could visit? Friends?"

Her remaining family was as foreign to her as the land of her mother's birth. And her friends, such as they were, consisted of a scowling Nick Wellington and the three women who had kidnapped her and forced her to buy that tiny bronze dress not an hour earlier.

But instead of admitting that, Genie said, "There's no way I'm leaving town now. I'm staying right here. You need me to figure out what's going on and who this jerk is so you can catch him and make him go away for a very, very long time.'' She glanced at Nick. ''You can leave if you want, though.''

She'd thought he might get offended at the suggestion, but she was wrong. He just stretched lazily and said, ''You've been trying to get me out of here since the day I walked in. If I didn't know better, I'd say you set this whole thing up just so you could get the equipment all to yourself.''

''Yeah. I attacked myself and then blew up my own car just so you'd go away. You've got a pretty inflated opinion of your own power, don't you, Beef?'' But she touched his arm as she said it, to let him know that she appreciated his attempt to lighten the admittedly dark mood. He caught her fingers in his own and, almost unwillingly, their hands intertwined.

''I'm not leaving you alone, understand?'' Nick brought their joined hands to his lips and she felt the kiss shimmer through her body until it coiled, throbbing and ready, in her stomach. ''Until this is over, we're a team.''

A team. The words glowed with promise if she ignored the time limit. Genie had never in her life been part of a team. The idea fascinated her. It worried her.

What if she did it wrong? What if she made a mistake?

Sturgeon cleared his throat and gathered his papers. ''Well, that's all I have for you today. Have you remembered anything more about your attack, Dr. Watson? If he mentioned on the phone that this was your second warning, it stands to reason he said something to you in the darkroom.''

As if she wouldn't have told him that first thing. Genie shook her head. ''Nothing more than a few impressions. I think I remember the darkness and the red lights warming up. Maybe a man behind me, breathing on my neck. A voice maybe? Nothing more than that."

Nick's fingers tightened. "A voice? Did you recognize it?

"Maybe. I think so. I don't know." Anger and fear and frustration beat at her, made her feel weak. "I don't remember. I can't remember. This has never happened to me before. I can *always* remember things." *It's who I am.*

"Don't worry about it, Dr. Watson. It's completely normal to suppress the memory of an event as traumatic as this. It's your brain's way of protecting itself."

"It has no right," she muttered, and Nick let go of her hand. She felt like crying for no good reason.

"What about hypnosis? Do you think that would help?" Nick's voice sounded very far away, as did Sturgeon's rumble as he replied that it might, but wasn't admissible in most situations if it came to a trial.

She shook her head, which was aching like fury again. "No hypnosis. I've tried it, and they tell me I'm not creative enough to be hypnotized."

There had been a pre-Archer frat party at college. She had been fifteen and desperate to fit in—so desperate that she'd pretended that the mesmerism had worked and she'd been programmed to cluck like a chicken. For a few weeks she'd remembered to flap her arms and say "bock, bock, bock" every time a classmate said the word *fellatio*. Then the novelty had worn off and Genie the Amazing Chicken Girl had gone back to being simply Genius Watson, geek.

Absently she wondered whether the same thing would happen this time. Once the madman was caught, would life go back to normal at the lab? Would Molly and Steph and Jill smile politely in the halls and call her Dr. Watson? Would they occasionally invite her along for a Friday night beer and seem relieved when she said she had work to do?

And what about Nick? Would he remember that she liked extra salt on her popcorn and none on her eggs? Would he knock on her door some night and see whether she was up for an evening of James Bond? Would he touch her in passing, unaware of the starburst of warmth that a simple hand on her shoulder could create?

Or would they fall back into their old roles and once again become Genius Watson and Beef Wellington, barely civil co-workers who fought over the vibrating incubator and ignored each other on the elevator?

Bingo.

Genie scowled at Nick, as irritated with him as if he had already left in search of prettier, more socially astute company.

"Well, if you can't be hypnotized, we'll just have to keep digging at those drug companies and looking at people connected to the Fenton's Ataxia project—including Mr. Dixon, however unlikely a suspect he might seem to Dr. Watson." Sturgeon stood. "The phones here and at your house are tapped, and a local uniform will make regular passes by your condo. I assume you'll be staying with Dr. Watson for the time being?''

The question was directed at Nick, who nodded, and Genie felt as if the Neanderthals had just agreed upon a strategy for defense of the cave. *You go hunt. I'll stay and protect woman from bear.*

Nobody ever thought to ask the woman what she thought about the arrangement—except that in this case, the arrangement suited the woman just fine.

And that realization was as unsettling as the thought of a dead man floating in Boston Harbor.

Nick tapped his fingers impatiently on the desk and glanced at Genie. She had been silent for too long and it made him edgy. She was either processing that foolish scene earlier when he'd flipped out because she'd gone shopping with the girls—something she'd never done before, and why pick today to start?—or she was worrying about the faceless terror that waited outside somewhere...or most likely she was trying to think of a reason why he shouldn't stay with her.

Besides the obvious one that he wasn't sure he could spend another night in that condo without putting his hands on her.

Sturgeon took his index cards and left after assuring the two scientists that there would be regular police patrols of the lab area and increased security in the garage where Nick's Bronco was parked. Genie paled at that last piece of information.

''You don't think...''

''Of course not,'' Sturgeon assured her. ''He has no way of knowing that Dr. Wellington is involved, and no reason to wish him ill.'' Nobody mentioned that Randy Baines hadn't been involved, either, and he'd ended up dead. "The patrols are simply a pre-caution—one that has been fully supported by the hospital, I might add."

"The hospital's paying for the patrols and the ga-rage security?" Nick wondered how badly Leo had squealed over the expense. The Head Administrator hated spending money on "unnecessary expendi-tures." "Why? Did something else happen? I'm sur-prised they're moving so fast." He shot an apologetic glance at Genie. "Her car wasn't on hospital prop-erty, and they've never been quick to react to things like this."

"There was an incident at the Eye Center the day before yesterday," Sturgeon allowed. He looked moderately embarrassed. "An office was broken into and a computer, some personal items, and several files were stolen."

Nick frowned. "That's the same day Genie was attacked. And this is the first we're hearing of this?"

Sturgeon coughed. He was definitely looking put out. "Yes. Well, because the Eye Center is on the opposite side of Boston General, it is the responsibil-ity of the Theater precinct, not Chinatown, and Peters and I didn't get the information until earlier today. We're checking into it, but it doesn't seem related."

"Two incidents at the same hospital on the same day and they're not related?" Genie seemed to find that as unbelievable as Nick did. "What office was broken into? I have files at several departments over there."

Sturgeon added a note to the growing pile and scowled. "You can be sure I'll find out. For now, let's concentrate on what we know about this case—

that it's connected to your Fenton's project. That's my job.'' Sturgeon leveled a finger at Nick and Genie. ''Your job is to stay safe.''

He made it to the door before he turned around and added, ''And it sure would help if Dr. Watson could remember what happened in that darkroom.''

GENIE STOOD IN THE sterile white hallway and curled her fingers into sweaty palms. Her stomach churned sluggishly and the fluorescent lights stabbed into her eyes and made her head spin and hurt at the same time.

Nick's office door, with its Face of Erectile Dysfunction poster, was slightly ajar and she knew the room was empty. Nick had followed Sturgeon downstairs, presumably to have more ''man talk'' without ''worrying the little lady.''

Molly and Steph had cleared the last of the stragglers out of Genie's lab, and Nick's side of the floor was equally deserted. When had it gotten to be quitting time? Genie glanced at her watch and was surprised to find that it was past six o'clock.

She was alone.

The lid of the developer stood open and the big machine was silent. Though Jonesy, Boston General's fix-it wizard, had been there that morning, the repairs would take at least another day and would involve the ordering of expensive brushes and rollers to rebuild the developer's guts. A faint smell of chemicals still hung in the hallway, overlain with that of the cleaning solutions used to wash away all signs of Genie's attack. Or so she hoped.

Because it was time to go back into the little room to see what memories it held.

She took a deep breath and put her hand on the light-lock door. What would she find in there? An enemy? A stranger? She thought of ice-blue eyes and shivered. A friend? Or nothing? What if she found nothing in there? No images, no memories, nothing.

Then she would know that her brain had well and truly failed her for the first time in her life. And in a way, that was the scariest thought of all.

"We going in?"

Genie jumped a mile and let out a little squeak. She'd been so caught up in arguing with her brain that she hadn't noticed Nick's arrival—but there he stood. At her shoulder. Handsome. Masculine.

Big Game.

Rubba-thump, rubba-thump. Pushing aside thoughts of hopeless fantasies, glad for his presence at her back, she spun the door so it would let her into the lock, then made sure that the outside switch was flipped up and the fluorescent lights were on in the little room. *Rubba-thump, rubba-thump.* She spun the door the other way and stepped into the developer room for the first time since she'd been carried out. The door rumbled behind her and Nick let himself through.

As she scanned the brightly lit, sparkling-clean room, Genie idly wondered how they had managed to get a stretcher out through the light lock. Then she recognized that thought for what it was: her rebellious brain's way of avoiding the real issue.

"Focus," she told it, and stared hard at the stain-less-steel sink at the end of the narrow room. There was a row of cabinets to the left, high shelves where they stored the film cassettes and the unexposed films, a waist-high counter where dark work could be done and a set of lower cabinets where the heavy bottles of developer chemicals were stored.

There was a fine layer of grit here and there, and Genie had watched enough forensics programs on TV to guess that it was fingerprinting powder. "They took prints and DNA samples?"

She felt Wellington nod at her back—felt it in the swirl of heavy air and the heat that trickled along her spine. "No real info from the prints yet, and the DNA is only good if there's a suspect to compare it with."

"No kidding. My lab does a little work for the forensics lab, remember?" But her idle remark held little sting as Genie tried to put herself back in time two days.

The room was cleaner than she'd ever seen it, and that in itself was eerie. She couldn't remember the attack, and the room didn't remember it, either.

It might never have happened at all.

But her stomach gave a little flutter at the sight of a pair of bandage scissors on the floor beneath the sink. She must remember them, but why? What had they done? Had he held them to her throat and whispered hot promises and heavy threats? Had she waved them around in the red blackness, trying to defend herself?

What had happened?

Suddenly cold in the close little space, Genie wrapped her arms around herself and shivered. It was too silent in the room. Too bright. She rocked herself and felt the unfamiliar bite of failure.

"I can't remember."

It almost broke Nick to see her standing there, holding herself as though she was the only person she'd ever been able to depend on. She closed her eyes in defeat, and that was enough to propel him the single step it took to close the distance between them.

She was shaking. Maybe they both were. He murmured nonsense words into her hair as she burrowed against his chest and held on tight. He boosted her up onto the waist-high counter and let her cling. Let himself soothe.

Three days ago Dr. Eugenie Watson had been nothing more to him than a worthy opponent in the Battle of the Thirteenth Floor, a woman whose reputation for utter brilliance and cool standoffishness was hard to deny when she wore old-lady clothes to work and turned down every social invitation sent her way. And a woman whose annoying habits were hard to ignore when his every breath was greeted by a pithy memo and a pointed complaint.

Now, in just seventy-two short hours, Genie Watson had become a whole new person to Nick. She was tough and resourceful, sweet and sexy and shy. And though Nick still didn't want the complication of a woman in his life—particularly this one—he couldn't seem to stop himself from touching her. Wanting her.

One of her narrow hands left his wrist to stroke his hair, his neck, then slide down to his shoulder and clench. He winced involuntarily when she touched the raw, singed place on his back. She made a small sound of distress and sat up, framing his face in her hands. "I hurt you. I'm sorry."

The burn pulsed thickly with the surge of blood through his body, and when she lightly traced the sore place with her fingertips, Nick couldn't tell whether the sensation that rocked through him was pleasure or pain.

It was simply everything.

The sweet torture continued as her fingers stroked the small scrape on his chin where he'd whacked the sidewalk after her car exploded, taking away the hurt and leaving flames behind. Her face was so close that he couldn't see the line of stitches marching across her brow, couldn't see the dark bloom of bruises on her cheek and chin. He could see only the liquid silver of her eyes boring into his.

Then her lips touched him, kissing away the pain in his shoulder and face and creating a new ache deep in his soul. He closed his eyes and felt the whisper of her lips travel across his cheek to the bridge of his nose, from the corner of his mouth to his temple.

He couldn't, shouldn't, *wouldn't* take advantage of her. She was scared. Vulnerable. And he was her protector. In any other circumstance she wouldn't have looked his way. She was destined for greatness, for Nobel prizes and groundbreaking research, not for a pedestrian biochemist who had left his mother and sister behind and saved himself. Not for a man who knew from experience that he made a better scientist than husband.

It wasn't lust. It was gratitude. That was all. But it didn't feel like gratitude when her mouth cruised back down and her tongue lightly, tentatively, traced the seam of his lips.

"Nick?" Her whisper was barely a breath but it

echoed in the tiny room, a sibilant hiss of things that waited for them in the dark.

"Nick. I know that this will be over soon, that they'll find this guy and things will go back to the way they were before, but will you do me a favor and kiss me? Just once, now. So I'll have new memories of this room, good ones rather than bad."

She leaned closer and traced her tongue across his lips again, an uncertain touch that made him wonder in his foggy brain just how many men she'd kissed before and whether they'd been both blind and stupid to let her go.

"Kiss me, Nick. Just once, so I know what it's like."

He could barely comprehend what she was saying, he was so caught up in the feel of her mouth hovering near his. Her scent spilled around him, drowning out the sharp tang of bleach and developer chemicals. He shouldn't. Couldn't.

"Genie, I—" *Shouldn't. Couldn't. Wouldn't.*
Will.

When he started to speak again, she covered his mouth with her own, slid her tongue between his lips, and he was lost. Utterly, irrevocably lost.

On a groan of surrender he slid his palms from her hips to her shoulders and stepped into the welcoming pocket between her knees, only peripherally aware that as she wrapped her calves around him the sensible brown skirt hiked up to her waist.

Muscles so tight he thought he might crack, Nick returned only as much as she gave, for in the hesitant little darts of her tongue and the fluttering motions of her hands at his shoulders, he knew that though she

might have had a lover in the past, she had not been
well served by him. But even the thought of Genie in
the arms of another man was enough to irritate Nick
and he unintentionally deepened the kiss, sliding her
forward on the counter until their bodies were flush
against each other and he felt the firm globes of her
breasts press against his chest and her secret softness
cradle him below.

She made a wordless sound and he pulled back,
fearing that it was too much, too fast. But she followed him with another murmur, cupping his face in
her gentle hands and sliding with him into that deep,
wet darkness where dreams spin out and reality is
lost. For though she kissed like an innocent, she tasted
like pure sin, rich and dark with promises and secrets.
And as the flavor seeped into Nick's soul, he thought
that he might never get enough of her.

Alarm bells went off in his head.

Whoop, whoop, whoop.

This is Watson we're talking about, he told himself.
*Genius Watson. Remember Pain-in-the-Butt Watson?
You're supposed to be protecting her, not mauling
her.* He groaned when he realized he had both hands
wrapped firmly around Pain-in-the-Butt Watson's
butt, pulling her even tighter against the place where
every drop of hot, screaming blood in his body
seemed to have collected.

She made a sexy purring noise in the back of her
throat and slid her lips from his throat to his ear.

For a novice she learned really, *really* quickly, and
Nick almost whimpered when the alarms rang more
loudly in his head, almost drowning out his own

groan when she traced the outside of his ear with her tongue.

Whoop! Whoop! Whoop!

"What the hell?" Genie pulled away from him and frowned over his shoulder, not meeting his eyes as she cocked her head as if listening for something.

Had she heard the bells, too?

Whoop! Whoop! Whoop!

And that was when Nick realized that the warning bells weren't in his head.

They were in the lab.

Chapter Nine

"It's the freezer alarms!" Genie pushed Nick aside with a two-handed shove and jumped off the counter. She lurched awkwardly when she landed and he noticed that one of her sensible brown shoes had fallen off. She kicked the other away and bolted for the light lock.

"Wait!" He practically slammed her out of the way, pausing to grab her arm before she fell. "I'm going first."

If this was a ruse to get Genie to run into the lab in a panic, then her little friend was going to be in for a surprise. Nick grabbed the developer's pipe wrench—a new one donated by the maintenance man since the police had taken the old one as evidence—and snuck out the rotating door.

Stealth was difficult when the door insisted on announcing their actions with a loud *rubba-thump, rubba-thump,* and Nick leaped into the hallway with the pipe wrench held high, ready to swipe it at the head of any crazed rapist-murderer who might be lying in wait.

The hallway was deserted.

"Okay, Genie, you can come out. It's clear." Nick turned to help her through the light lock and almost ran her over. She was right on his heels. Big surprise.

"Come on, I'm pretty sure it's the ultralow freezers in the main lab." Without waiting for her big protector with his pipe wrench, Genie pattered down the hallway in her nylon-clad feet.

"Genie?" Nick called, but she didn't turn around, giving him a nice view of a single strip of soft-looking satin flanked by two perfectly round, perfectly proportioned cheeks. He tried again, catching her just before she passed through the thankfully deserted reception area. "Dr. Watson?"

"What? Are you coming or not?"

He caught up to her and gave her a friendly pat on one panty-hose-covered buttock. "I'd suggest you pull your skirt down before maintenance gets here."

While she was wrestling the staid brown material back down around her knees, Nick slid into the lab with his weapon at the ready.

GENIE PAUSED AT THE threshold and peered around Nick's wide shoulders. The big room was empty except for the marching rows of lab benches, the crouching condors of fume hoods, and the lurking pieces of equipment that looked like something from the set of *Moonraker.*

Usually she adored being in the lab alone at night. She loved wandering from bench to bench and checking on her techs' progress, loved touching the big machines and thinking about all the lives they could save if only the silly humans asked the right questions.

But tonight the lab didn't feel peaceful in its lone-liness. It felt unhappy. Menacing. *Whoop, whoop, whoop!* The shadows that clouded the far reaches of the room were murky and Genie could imagine some-one hiding there dressed in green scrubs and blood.

Nick's solid presence at her side was a comfort if she ignored what had just happened between them. She couldn't believe she had forced him to kiss her. Couldn't believe how much she had enjoyed it and how much she wanted to repeat the experiment, and how utterly, unbelievably stupid that was. She had a fleeting urge to run downstairs—barefoot or not—get in her car and drive north until she ran out of gas or got to Canada, whichever came first.

But she couldn't do that because she didn't have a car anymore.

The alarm bells shrilled louder as they neared the cross aisle where the ultralow freezers sat. Seven feet tall, with enough armor to survive almost anything except a direct nuclear attack, the freezers stood in a row, normally silent guardians of the frozen samples they held within them—the collective work it had taken Genie and her employees almost five years to assemble.

Whoop! Whoop! Whoop!

Nick opened the door to the aisle and the alarms screamed in response. Any minute now Boston Gen-eral's Equipment Response Team would storm into the lab, ready to repair the broken equipment or to move the samples to another freezer if there was no hope of a quick fix.

Her wrench-wielding protector seemed paralyzed in the doorway so Genie poked him in the ribs and tried to peer around him. She gasped when she caught a glimpse of the hallway beyond.

Oh, no. Please no.

''He didn't.'' Genie pressed her aching forehead against Nick's solid, warm shoulder. ''Please tell me he didn't.''

Not the samples. Please, not the samples!

''Sorry, Genie. He did. God— I'm…I'm so sorry. Just look at this place.''

Two of the three freezers stood open, their contents strewn around with malicious disregard. The neat cardboard boxes that held hundreds upon hundreds of pellets painstakingly collected over five years were opened, crushed, and the small plastic tubes within had been ground underfoot.

The DNA of more than ten thousand people suffering from Fenton's Ataxia, Gray's Glaucoma, Humboldt's Dystrophy, and a handful of other diseases lay in melting smears on the linoleum floor of Genie's lab.

A bag of frozen cow's eyes she'd ordered for a forgotten experiment lay near Genie's foot and she had the sudden mad urge to kick those leering spheres across the room and to scream bloody murder. She stepped further into the aisle and when Nick tried to gather her close in comfort, she slapped him away.

''Don't coddle me now, Wellington. I'm in no mood for it. Who does this guy think he is?'' Her voice was starting to rise in volume as the anger that had simmered inside her erupted in an overdue fit of temper. ''He trashed my samples!''

She dropped to her knees and plucked up a few of

the crushed boxes, finding only a handful of DNA pellets intact in each one.

"Look at this. Do you see what he's done to my pellets? Five years it's taken me to collect all these families. Five years, four technicians, three clinical coordinators, two graduate students..." Inanely she heard the words *and a partridge in a pear tree* playing in her head, yet more rebellion from her formerly well-behaved brain. She snarled and stood, dropping the broken boxes amid the rubble on the floor. It was then that she noticed a single empty tube lying on the floor. It was labeled with a single word: Marilynn.

Whoop, whoop, whoop!

Genie's head throbbed harder at the continued shrill of the thaw alarms that were set to sound when the interior temp of the ultralow freezers went above fifty degrees below zero. She stabbed at a pair of red buttons and the noise ceased.

The silence was deafening.

She stooped and picked up the sad little tube. Slipped it into her pocket.

"Are you okay?" Nick's question was quiet, gentle, and meant to help, but Genie found a bitter-tasting humor in it.

She laughed shortly. "Yeah. Just ducky. In the space of three days I've been attacked, knocked out, practically raped, had my car blown up with someone else in it, gotten the heck scared out of me by a totally strange phone call, and now most of my working DNA library has been destroyed. I'm doing just great."

Staring at the bag of cow eyeballs that were staring back, Genie felt a bubble of hysteria rise and threaten to break free, but she beat it back with sheer will-power. She put both hands over her eyes in a childish attempt to block out the sight of the open freezer doors. "And it's only Wednesday. I need a vacation. When this is over, let's go to Disney, okay? I've always wanted to go to Disney."

She'd meant it as a joke, but that didn't stop it from stinging when Nick turned her to face him. Looked down at her with serious eyes. "Genie, I—"

"Never mind. Bad idea." She held up a hand to stop him, though on top of the anger over the destruction of her lab, it felt as though something was cracking in her chest. "I know kissing you in the darkroom was my idea. And I know that when this is over, it's over. You don't have to worry about me. I'm good at being on my own."

Rather than looking pleased that she'd relieved him from any awkward explanation, Nick looked pissed. "Damn it, Genie. Don't—" At that moment, the Equipment Response Team arrived with a clatter.

"We're here. What's wrong with the freezers? Holy sh—" A string of expletives followed the team's entrance and Nick stepped back, creating a distance between them that seemed to stretch for miles.

She could still feel his hands on her shoulders. Still taste him on her lips, a heady combination of vanilla coffee and man. And she wished it could've been different between them.

Genie took a deep breath and tried to wrap the tattered cloak of Dr. Eugenie Watson, M.D., Ph.D. around her shoulders, but it didn't seem to fit quite right anymore. "There's been a break-in. Or at least

I think he broke in.'' She was beginning to think the bastard had a passkey. He certainly seemed able to waltz in and out of the building on a whim.

The response team shuffled from foot to foot. They were used to blown fans, frayed power cords and computer malfunctions, not mayhem. They didn't seem sure of what to do and they milled about uncertainly, all except for a single shadowy figure that Genie noticed at the outskirts of the E.R.T. "George, what are you doing here?"

Dixon shrugged and his eyes flickered from Genie to Nick and back. He smirked. "I was just passing by when I saw these guys hustling up to your floor. I figured I'd tag along and see if you'd had yourself another spill." He glanced down at the scattered tubes and broken boxes on the floor, nudged the melting cow's eyes with a toe. "Seems as though you don't need me, though. Not unless you've been storing radioactive samples in the ultralows again."

Wouldn't he just love to write that up? Genie shook her head and felt her brain swim. "Nope. You're out of luck, George. Nothing to see here, so move along."

He grumbled and left, and the E.R.T. workers coughed and looked at each other. Their leader said, "Do you want us to help clean up?" and the others nodded, surprising Genie, since that wasn't their job.

"No. Thanks, but no. The freezers are fine. The alarms sounded because the doors had been left open long enough to bring them past temp." She paused and looked at the destruction, feeling that sick, unfamiliar anger churning in her stomach. "I think we should leave this stuff the way it is and call in the detectives."

"Already done." She hadn't noticed Nick speaking into the lab phone, but just a few more minutes passed before Sturgeon and Peters buzzed from the elevators to announce their arrival. They must have been in the neighborhood, just like George Dixon had been. Coincidence?

Genie scowled. She didn't believe in coincidences.

NICK NOTICED THAT GENIE was very quiet throughout the detectives's questioning and he sensed a maelstrom of emotions flickering through her—anger, frustration, helplessness, rage, despair, desire.

Anger at whoever was doing this. Frustration that the police seemed unable to make headway, unable to prevent the culprit's next move. Desire for the kisses that had begun in the darkroom to be continued in another place, at another time where there were fewer interruptions and no dangers from lurking shadows.

Darting a quick glance at her frozen face, Nick grimaced. It was also possible that she was numb with shock and he was projecting. She hadn't seemed particularly affected by those kisses a few minutes ago when she was explaining why it had been no big deal. The thought stung.

She was barely responsive as Sturgeon jotted notes on his index cards and devoured a steady stream of peppermints. The detective had graduated from sucking on the candies to outright crunching, and Nick wondered whether that boded well or ill for the case.

He feared the latter. Sturgeon and Peters seemed somewhat at a loss, and as they went through the routine of requesting the passkey logs from the main door and the sign in sheets from the front lobby, it was obvious they didn't expect to find anything out of the ordinary this time, either.

"We need to talk to all the employees on this floor." Sturgeon shuffled cards until he found the one he wanted and passed it to Nick.

On it were the names of his technicians, Genie's technicians, all the post docs and interns that worked on the floor. Nick hid the flinch. Logically, any one of the names could belong to the monster. Any one of the hardworking researchers he and Genie had hand picked over the years might be a killer.

And he didn't believe it for a damn minute.

"I think you're off track with that hypothesis, but if you're certain…" Nick shrugged, scribbled a few more names on the card and passed it back. "I'd add the maintenance and cleanup crews, as well as the Radiation Nazis. I know George Dixon looks clean, but he was right behind the response team when they arrived for the freezers. Said he'd been in the neighborhood."

Sturgeon nodded, added Dixon's name to the list, then shot a glance at Genie. "Not to sound foolish, Dr. Watson, but are you all right? You're awfully quiet."

She snorted. "Yeah, fine, thanks." But sitting in her office chair, kind of slumped down with her hair falling around her face and the top two buttons of her shirt undone, she looked tired. Defeated. Young.

Beautiful.

Nick fought the urge to kneel in front of her, to gather her in his arms and to promise her that he would make everything better. But how could he do that? He couldn't undo what had been done to her in the darkroom, couldn't bring Randy Baines back to life. And much as he might wish he had the power to do so, he could not go back and undo the destruction of her work. He could only watch as Genie sagged in the chair, her face a sickly pale color beneath the greening bruises and the spidery black stitches.

And remind himself that he didn't need another failed relationship, and that Genie and Lucille had more than a few things in common.

Complaints. Shopping.

Well, at least two things. Nick scowled and returned his attention to the detective.

"I think that's enough for tonight." Sturgeon pocketed the index cards and stood, apparently sensing that Genie was at the end of her rope. "Go home and get some sleep. There will be officers watching both the lab and your condo, and I'd suggest you let the machine pick up any calls you get tonight." He paused at the door and waited until Genie looked at him. "We're working on it, Dr. Watson. We'll get him. But I'm sure sorry we haven't got him yet."

She mustered a tired smile. "I know you're doing your best, Detective Sturgeon. We all are."

Sturgeon left after reminding them to assemble their various employees the next day for questioning. Nick watched him go and felt almost unbelievably tired at the thought of driving home.

"Good. He's gone. Let's get to work. Can you hand me that box over there?"

Surprised, Nick spun around and found Genie standing behind the desk, her face slightly flushed and her silver eyes glittering with purpose. "What?"

"That box over there. Pass it over." She turned to the rank of gunmetal-gray filing cabinets that took up one wall of her office and began pulling out fat files and piling them on the desk. Her movements were quick, almost frenetic, and as the tall stack on the desk grew, it tilted alarmingly and threatened to slide to the floor.

Nick grabbed a pair of cardboard boxes that had once held cell culture flasks made by Petrie Pharmaceuticals, and started loading the files into them. "What are we doing?"

"I'm taking a stand, that's what I'm doing. There's no way I'm going to let this schmuck ruin my lab, and I'm not going to be responsible for anyone else getting hurt." She dumped an armload of color-coded files into the second box. "He's in here—in one of the personnel files, or in one of the Fenton's families. He has to be in here somewhere, and I'm going to find him."

"How?"

"I'm a genius," she told him bitterly. "Haven't you heard? I'm Genius Watson. My IQ is off the charts. By the time I was five years old they ran out of ways to measure my aptitudes and my parents were so terrified of me they sent me to school year-round and paid attention to my refreshingly average brother." She yanked open another drawer and pulled out thirty or so blue files, which went into the second box.

"I was a freak. A child who could calculate undefined probabilities in her head while comparing the works of John Donne to Steinbeck out loud. Half of my teachers resented me for knowing more than they did, half of the kids were convinced I escaped from Area 51.'' She shoved the box, which slid across the desk and would have fallen if Nick hadn't caught it on the way down.

"You're not a freak," he said quietly. "You're a beautiful woman."

"I'm a freak," she repeated mechanically as she dragged a soft suede jacket over her arms. "But so is whoever is doing this. He's evil. He's heartless. And he's smart—smarter than hospital security. Smarter than Sturgeon and Peters. But…" Her breath hissed out and her silver eyes snapped at Nick. "He's not smarter than me. And I'm going to get him."

Nick didn't bother to argue with her, because what was the point? She was absolutely right. Sturgeon and Peters were making only marginal headway, the bad guy was running circles around them, and given enough information Nick firmly believed that Genie could figure out who was behind all the incidents in their shared lab space. But she was wrong about one thing. She wasn't going to be doing it alone.

He hefted the two boxes easily and gestured with his chin for her to precede him out of the office. "Sounds good, Watson, except for one thing."

Braced for a fight, she merely arched a brow, then winced when the stitches pulled. "Which is?"

"*You're* not going to get him. *We* are."

Chapter Ten

You're *not going to get him*. We *are*.

Genie snuggled down in the passenger seat of Nick's Bronco as she replayed the words in her head. As much as she wanted to protect her new friends, she couldn't help but feel better that Nick insisted on helping.

It was raining and the streetlights shone yellow-orange on the glistening black road, softened by the glowing green lights on the Bronco's dash. Exhausted, Genie let her eyelids drift down and was lulled by the hiss of tires on wet pavement, the *lub-dub* heartbeat of the windshield wipers and the soft murmur of classic rock on the radio.

She let her lips trace the words of the song about finding someone to love.

She opened her eyes partway, hoping Nick would think her still asleep. He drove easily, gliding through the city like a native even though she knew from office gossip that he'd been born in California. For all his easy popularity, Genie noticed he rarely talked about himself and idly wondered why.

Against the streetlights, his profile should have

been forbidding with its aggressive brow and prominent nose, but she found it comforting in its very fierceness.

Nick Wellington was a M-A-N man, as Marilynn used to say. She would usually follow that statement by patting Genie with a trembling hand and saying, *You'll understand that someday, Eugenie. When you're older.*

Well, it had taken more than ten years, but Genie finally understood what an M-A-N man was. He was sitting right beside her, just a touch away.

As if he had heard her thoughts, Nick glanced over. They were stopped at a red light and the engine hummed a steady counterpoint to the ping of the rain on the roof. Genie forced herself to breathe evenly, though her heart thumped when he continued to look at her, his cool blue eyes lingering on her with an expression of—what? What was he thinking as he sat waiting for the light to change?

What was he feeling when he lifted his hand to her cheek? Was he thinking about protecting her? About solving the mystery so they could both go back to their separate lives? Or was he thinking something else?

Was he remembering their kiss in the darkroom? Had it even registered on the Richter scale of his life?

Probably not.

Genie sighed and closed her eyes firmly as the Bronco accelerated onto the highway and the song switched to something slow and melancholy. She was not Cinderella to be rescued from loneliness by a handsome Primary Investigator, or Snow White and seven very short lab techs. She was Genius Watson.

And nobody wrote fairy tales about geniuses.

But then again, nobody tried to kill them, either.

ALTHOUGH NICK WAS pretty sure she'd been faking sleep most of the way home, Genie was out cold by the time the security gates swished shut behind the Bronco and he parked close to the front entrance.

"Genie? Genie, wake up. We're here."

She murmured and shifted, her eyelashes fluttering up and down, dark smudges against the fine paleness of her cheek. "Where? What?"

He popped the back hatch and hauled out the boxes of files, throwing his coat over the top of them to keep out the soaking rain. "We're home. Well, we're at my home anyway." He left the boxes on the top step and went back for her. "Come on in before the rain does any more damage to your jacket."

Urging her up the stairs, he dug through his pockets for the archaic key ring that had come with the house. When the heavy double doors were unlocked, he kicked them open and dragged the damp cardboard boxes across the threshold. Genie didn't follow.

"Something wrong?" He looked back through the door to see her standing in the rain with her hair plastered around her face and the shoulders of her suede coat turning dark. "Genie, what is it?"

"Where are we?"

"I told you, my house." He ducked back out, grabbed her by the arm and half carried her inside. Obviously that head injury was having more of a lingering effect than he'd thought.

"This is your *house?* This isn't a house, it's a bloody mansion. Please tell me you rent a room or

two in the back wing.'' She stood stiffly in the marble
entryway while he peeled the sopping jacket off her
shoulders. The cut-glass chandelier sprayed droplets
of light across her agitated features.

''Sorry. It's mine. My grandfather's lawyers said it
was a good investment, and the gates and the alarm
systems passed muster with my father's advisors
when he was running for president. He was getting
death threats at the time—big surprise—and he ordered my sister and I to have bodyguards. I compro-
mised with this place instead and I've been pretty
happy with it. It's big and I don't use most of it, but
there's plenty of room for visiting fellowship students
to stay, and…'' Nick trailed off. He was babbling.

Genie continued to stand and stare, and for the first
time in a long while, Nick felt awkward about his
money. When he'd been a child it had set him apart
from everyone else, just as Genie had been different
from the other kids. At M.I.T., then Boston General,
he'd been judged on his work, not his trust fund. The
one glaring exception had been his marriage to Lucille, which he'd realized later was one of the few
things he'd ever done that the Senator would've ap-
proved of.

That in itself should've told him just what a bad
idea it had been. But in his own defense, he'd thought
she loved him when all she'd really loved was his
name and his wallet.

He was an heir in his own right—he controlled his
grandfather's estate and was grateful he'd never need
the Senator's money—and he'd assumed it was common knowledge at Boston General. There had certainly been the usual complement of eyelash-

fluttering, giggling women asking him out when he
first accepted the Primary Investigator position at
BoGen and moved onto Genie's floor. But apparently
the gossip had missed her, or else she'd never really
thought about Dr. Beef Wellington and where he
might live.

He preferred the first option.

"Genie," he began gently, reminding himself that
she was having a helluva week and he shouldn't add
to it by being insulted that she didn't like his house.
"I know it's big, but it's safe. There's a gate with a
manned guardhouse at the entry to the complex,
alarms on every window and door, patrols every hour
or so, and a fence around the backside of those woods
over there." He gestured into the night that was visible through the sliding doors at the end of the hall.

Usually he hated the precautions, chafed at the
gates and the alarm codes and the occasional German
shepherd bark in the darkness, but tonight he was
grateful for them. He hadn't consciously turned the
Bronco past her neighborhood and toward his, but
once the thought had taken root it made immediate
sense.

He wanted her safe, wanted them both in a place
where they could relax for a few hours, catch up on
some sleep and look at those boxes of records she
seemed certain held the answer. He wasn't so sure of
that, but he was positive that he wanted to protect
her. So he'd brought her home.

"Scrow mreorw row!" A thin tomcat with odd
tufts of hair growing out of his ears appeared from
the direction of the kitchen, aimed a filthy look in

Nick's direction, and sauntered into the living room with his scruffy tail held high.

And miracle of miracles, Genie relaxed. Nick figured that to her, a house couldn't be that repulsive if it had an ugly cat in it.

She took a couple of steps in the direction the cat had taken, then turned to look at Nick. "Yours?" He nodded. "What's his name?"

Nick grinned. "Q."

She laughed. "Between your pets and mine, we can do most of a Bond movie. We just need a secret agent." She sobered. "And a villain."

Both of them looked over at the sagging cardboard boxes filled with colored file folders.

"Yeah." Nick pushed an impatient hand through his hair and listened to his cat curse him from the kitchen. "I guess I'd better feed him. You want anything?"

"Crunchies or wet food?" She grinned tiredly, then sobered. "I'm kidding. I'd love a cup of coffee if you've got some, or anything with lots of caffeine. I'm exhausted and I've got a lot of files to go through. Where can I work?"

There were deep shadows below her eyes and her skin looked almost transparent where it stretched tautly across the bones of her face. Nick wanted to scoop her up, wrap her in something warm and fluffy, and sit next to her on the couch watching television until they both fell asleep. But that wouldn't get them any closer to the truth. He understood the restless energy he saw working at the ends of her busy fingers, the need to do something, anything, that would help end the madness that swirled around their lab.

It was still hard for him to conceive that they were talking about Genie's life, but the faceless baddie had killed twice already—Randall Baines and the hit man in the Harbor, O'Shea. Nick didn't think he was done yet—not until he stopped Genie's research for good.

And that was unacceptable.

Nick pointed up the wide, carpeted stairs. "You're soaking wet. Why don't you get warm and we'll have a bite to eat before we look at the files. The master bedroom's the third door on the left. There's a bathroom where you can take a shower, and I'll leave a towel and some clothes out for you." There were three other bathrooms in the house—or four, he couldn't quite remember—but Nick wanted her to use his bedroom. His shower.

His brain flicked to another night, another shower, and his body heated at the thought. Hardened.

Pulsed.

Some of Nick's inner turmoil must have shown on his face because when he looked at Genie she was staring back at him, her eyes liquid pools of molten silver. Beneath the damp cotton of her white shirt, her nipples peaked and he bit back a groan.

That was not the kind of protection he intended to give her. But something about her called to him, challenged him. Filled up the lonely places with irritation and sharp, spiky needs.

He almost took a step toward her but forced himself to stop. He'd been careless once already that day, kissing her in the little developer room while a killer rampaged through their shared space. He had been distracted and her work had paid the price. Next time, it might be Genie herself.

It would not happen again. He had to be smarter, faster, better than the others. At least his father had been right about that.

So he kept his arms at his sides, made his face into that of a concerned friend and shooed her up the stairs like a mother hen.

He'd never felt less motherly in his life and was almost absurdly glad when the phone rang.

He grabbed the receiver. "Wellington."

"I called Genie's house and there was no answer," Steph said without preamble. "I started to get worried that she was in trouble, but then I thought I'd see whether you had her before I panicked."

"Were you worried or nosy?" But he grinned as he asked. He appreciated the way the women had reached out to Genie. Well, he'd appreciated it after he got over being mad that they went shopping— *shopping* of all things—when Genie's life was in danger.

"I take it that means she's with you?" came the dry reply and Nick grinned. He'd always liked Steph, though until recently she'd worn more invisible Keep Away signs than Dixon's toxic dump of an office. He hoped this new guy deserved her.

"Yeah, she's with me. Anything else, Mom?"

Steph's laugh tinkled down the line. "No, that's it for now. Just be kind, okay? She's had a rough week, and I get the feeling she's not quite up to Nick Wellington set on 'stun.'"

Then, as he was trying to decide whether or not he wanted to know what she meant by that, Steph said a quick goodbye and hung up.

Trying to imagine setting himself on "stun" and

not sure if the image was good or bad, Nick followed Q's howls into the kitchen, planning to force-feed Genie if necessary before they set to work on the files. Ignoring the soggy boxes of folders for the moment, he lit the burner under a pan of canned soup, started a trio of grilled-cheese sandwiches, then remembered he had promised Genie clean towels and dry clothes.

He grinned at the threshold of his bedroom. Who would've thought that Genius Watson was a shower singer? And a particularly bad one at that. He winced as she missed a high note by more than a couple standard deviations. At least she was feeling well enough to attempt to sing—whatever it was.

But as he put the finishing touches on their simple dinner, Nick found himself humming the refrain she had so mangled. It was something about finding someone to love.

He'd thought he'd been in love with Lucille, but after a year of failing to figure out what exactly she wanted when she complained, he'd decided that he made just as poor a husband as the Senator in his own less violent way. And when she'd left and the only emotion he'd felt was a sort of tired relief, Nick had called his mother, hoping she could help him understand.

But she'd been at the hairdresser's, and then several fund-raisers, and then Hawaii, and hadn't called him back for almost three weeks. By that time, Nick had decided he didn't care after all.

If that was love, he could do without it.

After arranging the soup and sandwiches on the butcher block table in the kitchen—he'd only used the dining room once since he moved in—Nick started coffee brewing and tried to decide whether white or red wine went better with tomato soup and grilled cheese.

While his body went through the motion of un-corking the selected vintage, his mind floated upstairs to the shower. The lyrics echoed in his brain just as Genie's remembered flavor taunted him, making the first swallow of hundred-dollar-a-bottle Chardonnay taste flat and lifeless.

"She'll be gone soon and we can get back to our real lives," he said to the ugly white cat, trying to make it sound appealing.

Q flicked his tail and walked away.

THE BRASS-ACCENTED bathroom smelled like Nick, masculine and commanding, and the shower was ten times better than hers. With a groan, Genie set the nozzle on high and let the powerful jets beat the fa-tigue from her shoulders and neck while she kept her stitches dry. She sang a snatch or two of the song that had been playing in the car, more because it was run-ning through her head than because she felt like sing-ing.

Until she'd moved into the condo she hadn't even known she liked singing in the shower. She suspected from the complete absence of songbirds at her bath-room window that she was pretty awful, but she didn't care. At least she usually didn't, but as Genie emerged from the steaming bathroom and found the sweatpants and shirt he'd left, she fervently hoped Nick hadn't heard her.

She glanced around as she pulled on the sweats and tried not to wonder who they belonged to.

The bedroom looked like Nick, with an unmade wrought-iron bed and random horizontal storage of clothing and accessories strewn across a simple woven rug in geometric patterns of blue and green. Like the bathroom, it smelled like him, and she inhaled and resisted the urge to crawl into his bed to sleep for a day or two.

"Not yet," she told herself sternly as she shook out the folded shirt. "We have things to do before bed." She glanced at the rumpled covers and felt her face heat and was grateful that he wasn't there to see, and amended, "We have *work* to do."

And a killer to catch.

He'd left her a soft dress shirt, one that had seen many washings and rippled from her fingers in a flow of ivory cotton. She shrugged into it and buttoned it up the front, wallowing in the feel of the cloth next to her bare skin and the smell of the man that tickled her nostrils.

Nick. She'd always thought it foolish when the girls in the dorm would crow over wearing their boyfriends' jackets, their letter sweaters or even T-shirts. Now she understood.

The cotton caressed her, brushed against her peaked nipples and touched her stomach slyly, sensuously, and she wrapped her arms around herself and breathed him in, imagined that her arms were his. *This* is what they had been talking about. This sense of rightness, of comfort.

Of belonging to someone, if only temporarily. And in extremely extenuating circumstances.

She hugged herself tighter and glanced at her reflection in the big mirror on the back of an open closet door. Nick's clothes hung in the closet, familiar yet not, and the image of a young woman looked back at her from the glass. Her hair was a rumpled, wet mass. Her face was a conglomeration of sickly bruises and stitches framing big, scared eyes. The dress shirt swallowed her whole, and the sweatpants that puffed down over her feet were too long, expensive, and belonged to someone else.

Genie might not know much about relationships, but she figured that a woman didn't leave clothes like that at a man's house unless she was very, very comfortable with him. She scowled and the woman in the mirror who was not Dr. Eugenie Watson frowned back.

"Temporary," she reminded herself. "This is only temporary, until the lab is safe again. Then it'll be back to Genius Watson and Beef Wellington and all this will be over."

She hugged herself tighter, damning the compulsion that had her turning her nose into the collar of the shirt and breathing deeply until the essence of Nick blotted out the faceless shadow that chuckled at the edge of her mind, hiding behind the locked door that contained her memories of the attack. "Time to work," she muttered, opening the bedroom door and stepping out into the hall.

If the bathroom and the bedroom were the Nick she knew, then the hallway and presumably the rest of the monstrous house belonged to the Nicholas Wellington the Third that she did not.

The hallway—approximately a quarter mile of burnished hardwood floor covered in an exquisite woven silk runner—fed into no fewer than twelve doors along its length before hooking a right-angle turn and disappearing into who knew where. It was lit by a series of glass sconces and hanging lights that recalled the enormous chandelier hanging in the football-field-size foyer.

Genie felt very scruffy, very small, and very, very out of place.

This was not the home of Beef Wellington, the drop-dead gorgeous Ph.D. who shared—or didn't as the case might be—her lab space and had come to her rescue once at the hospital, once in a Chinatown parking lot and once again in a room of screaming, empty freezers.

No, this was the home of Dr. Nicholas Wellington the Third, son of the gentleman from California and his rich wife.

Genie was just beginning to know Nick the researcher. She was coming to lean on Nick the protector. But this other Nick, the one he hid at home, flat out terrified her. Who was she to think that a man with all these opportunities might be interested in a geek like her?

It was laughable.

"Genie? Everything okay up there? I've got dinner on the table when you're ready." His voice floated up from below with an echo that reminded her of just how big the house was.

Just how far apart they were.

Since her feet were cold, Genie returned to Nick's bedroom and rummaged around until she found a clean pair of socks. It was odd that she felt no reservations searching his room for socks, but she could barely walk on the hallway runner. Once again fighting a deep desire to curl up on the bed and never come out ever again, she padded downstairs, keeping to the edge of the carpet so as not to mark it.

The foyer was just as big as she remembered it, but the cardboard boxes had been moved. She could see a little trail of rainwater spotting the tile and she followed it down the hall to the kitchen, which was done in marble and granite, a sinuous flow of stone countertop and natural wood accented in brass and copper.

It suited the Nick Wellington who moved easily between the built-in grill and the sturdy butcher-block table, arranging stoneware plates on square woven mats. This Nick wore casual tan pants and an expensive-looking white shirt open at the throat. She could just see the shape of the bandage on his shoulder where he'd been hurt. Was it just the day before? His hair was a dark wet slick across his forehead, making Genie wonder why he'd wanted her to use his personal shower when there was obviously at least one other.

Dull silver glinted at his wrist and Genie suddenly realized that the fake Rolex she had hooted over during one of their labware battles probably wasn't fake at all.

The room and the clothes suited the man. But who was he? Certainly not Beef Wellington, bane of her existence, nor Nick Wellington, the man who'd pushed her into a stinking gutter and shielded her with his own body.

This was Nicholas Wellington III, senator's son, heir to a fortune. And if Nick Wellington had been out of her league before, then there was no measuring the gulf that existed between plain little Genius Watson and the man who now stood before her.

Noticed her.

"Genie!" He appeared pleased to see her, but it was probably just good manners. "There you are. I see you found the clothes." His eyes traveled up and down her body and she refused to squirm, even when something bright and dangerous seemed to flare in the backs of his cool blue eyes. Something that only existed in her imagination, darkroom kisses aside.

"Yes, I found them. I—" *Love the shirt, hate the pants. Whose are they? Who is she? Do you care for her?* She shrugged helplessly. "Thanks."

Teeth gleamed quickly behind perfect lips. "The sweats belong to my sister, Shelly. She left them here the last time she visited."

Relief bubbled quickly, followed by a faint blush. "I didn't ask, did I?"

"Of course not." He gestured to the table. "Sit. Eat. I made comfort food—we deserve it." He held out a sturdy, surprisingly comfortable wooden chair and slid her into place once she was seated.

"Comfort food?" The scents of warm, buttery cheese sandwiches and tomato soup rose up and Genie almost hummed in appreciation. "Is that what this is?"

"Sure. At least it is for me. Mrs. Greta, our cook, would make it for me when I was sick. This or macaroni with hot dogs. Notice the warm cheese component? I think that's a requirement for comfort food. Hot cheese or chocolate or both." He sat down and his stockinged feet bumped against hers under the table. Rather than apologizing and moving his feet away, he pressed his toes to hers and left them there, as though they were holding hands. Holding feet. Whatever. "What about you?"

Caught up in the feel of his big toe making little circles on top of her left foot, Genie was slow to respond. "Huh?"

Oh, yeah, real genius at work. Stand back everyone, she might be getting ready to drool. In self-defense Genie jammed a spoonful of tomato soup into her mouth and almost yelped when it burned its way across her tongue and down her throat.

"I told you it was hot," he observed mildly, and Genie tried to remember when he'd said that. Probably right about the time she was debating whether he was playing footsie or scratching an itch on what he assumed was the table leg.

"I like it hot." She had meant the answer to be flip and to put them back on somewhat more stable ground, but in the wake of thousand-degree tomato soup, her voice was low, husky. Suggestive. His eyes flashed hard and bright and she took another hit of soup, hoping the pain would shock her back to her senses before she said or did something really, really stupid.

He muttered something unintelligible and she frowned and bit into the sandwich, closing her eyes in bliss as the taste of buttery toast and American cheese flooded her mouth. Fatty calories swooped across her tongue and she could practically feel them flooding her bloodstream with plump, happy lipids.

Maybe there was something to this comfort-food idea, after all. She smiled and hummed in pleasure at the next bite.

Nick made a muffled noise that sounded as though he might be in pain, but when she glanced at him in inquiry, his face was shuttered. "So what are we looking for in those boxes? The name of our bad guy lit up in neon letters? A scarlet M next to his name for Murderer?"

Genie shrugged. "No. I just want to go over the labs and the families in the Fenton's project to see if anything clicks. Not very logical, but I have to do *something* or I'll go crazy."

Nick brought a pair of coffee mugs to the table and added cream to hers, no sugar. Just the way she liked it. "Why not look at the other scientists first? He's got to have at least a little training in order to hit your lab where it hurts. And don't forget that he seems to be able to waltz in and out of the building at his convenience. That says 'researcher' to me, or at least 'radiation safety.'"

Genie was startled. She hadn't thought of that, which just went to show that she wasn't herself these days. "Well, I don't know about rad safety, but you might have a point about this person knowing more than a bit about the lab. Otherwise, how would he know that wrecking the developer and the DNA stocks would shut us down?"

Nick chewed thoughtfully and Genie realized he'd stolen half a sandwich from her plate. "But what's the goal? The motivation? Do you really think there's anything in those files that'll help?"

She shook her head and stood. "I don't know, but I've got to do something other than wait for Sturgeon and Peters. They seem competent, but they don't know the first thing about science."

"I think Peters is smarter than you give him credit for," Nick said. "But I agree that we should work at it from our side, too. Otherwise who knows what will happen next?"

Though neither said it out loud, they both knew that with the lab at a standstill, the only remaining targets would be the people who worked at the labs.

Or, more likely, Genie herself.

The fear and anger that had simmered most of the day erupted again and Genie kicked the soggy box with her sock-covered foot. "I hate this. I hate him." She kicked the box again, leaving a squishy indent on the side and jostling the piles of brightly colored folders.

Nick's fingers touched her shoulder, urged her to lean back against him, but she shook the desire away and knelt down next to the box while Q jumped in to investigate.

"Mreep prowr mreow!" The scruffy white tom bumped his head against her chin and she sighed.

"He's in here. I know he's in here. I can feel it— I just have to figure out who he is. I can do it." She wasn't sure if she was trying to convince the white cat, Nick or herself. "I'm a genius, haven't you heard? If anyone can figure it out, it should be me."

Nick didn't leave her alone as she'd expected him to do. He squatted down beside her on the floor. "It'll be us, Genius." And this time the nickname didn't sound as horrible as it usually did. "I'd say you've been on your own for way too long. This time you're going to have help whether you like it or not." He grabbed a handful of blue folders.

She grabbed them back.

"It's not like I don't appreciate the help," she began when he spluttered and tried to retrieve the files. She was not going to play tug-of-war with confidential information, so she hid them behind her back.

"Then let me help."

"I can't." She yanked them away from his seeking hands, reminded again of just how much bigger he was. Just how easily he could subdue her.

Bend her to his ways.

Whoa, not going there. Genie reined in her wayward thoughts and glared at Nick without much venom. "I can't let you go through these files. It's an ethics thing. Some of this family and genetic data is confidential. That's why I wouldn't give them to Sturgeon when he asked for them. Don't you remember that argument?"

"Well, yeah. But I'm a scientist. I didn't figure the rules applied."

"Nice try, but that only counts if you're a collaborator on the project, and even then the rules on what you can and can't share are pretty strict."

He perked up. "Well, I had planned on saving this for later..." He let the words trail off seductively and Genie felt a sliver of heat pierce her belly.

"...But I've been wanting to talk to you about collaborating with my lab on some candidate gene screens. We're finishing up a pair of big projects—the manuscripts are already written and submitted—and I was thinking..."

She tried not to feel the disappointment. He was talking about work. "Yes?" she prompted listlessly. "You were thinking?"

"That we should work together." His voice

dropped a notch and he leaned closer until they were almost huddled on top of each other between a pair of disintegrating cardboard boxes on the polished tiled floor of his amazing kitchen. "Collaborate." His voice grew rougher. "Work side-by-side. Shoulder to shoulder." She could swear he bumped her body with his. "Hip to hip."

"You—" Her voice shook for no good reason except that Nick Wellington, the M-A-N man of every woman's dreams, seemed to be coming on to her.

Or else he was only talking about work. The last thing she wanted to do was to find out which one it was by making a complete fool of herself.

She tried again. "You want to collaborate? You want to be—uh, *work* together after this is all over?"

He grinned, and that hot glint was back in his eyes. "Oh, yeah."

In self defense—because if they stayed on the floor nose-to-nose much longer she was going to kiss him. Genie stood and tucked her arms under each other, praying that he wouldn't notice how perky her nipples had suddenly become under the soft cotton of her borrowed shirt. "Well, okay. I guess we could do it. Uh, collaborate, that is."

Always the gentleman, Nick stood when she did, but he didn't give her any more space than before. He held out his hand as though daring her to take it.

"Well then, Dr. Watson. I guess that makes us partners, doesn't it?"

She stared at the hand—blunt and capable, with a dark smudge of blue nuclear stain on the thumb. Her own hand—pale and small in comparison—crept up to take his and the shock when they touched was almost palpable, as if she had just stuck her finger in the buffer well of one of the big gel boxes.

He closed his fingers over hers, tightening his grip when she would have pulled away. "Partners?" he asked again and she nodded, wondering why she felt as if she was agreeing to so much more than an association between neighboring labs.

"Yes, Dr. Wellington. Partners."

Chapter Eleven

"Remind me what we're looking for again?" Nick rubbed a hand across his burning eyes and rolled his neck for the hundredth time, trying to ease the kinks.

Genie took a sip of coffee and grimaced, either because it was stone cold or because her taste buds were as sick of coffee as his. "I don't even know anymore. I thought I did when we started, but that was three hours and two pots of coffee ago. Now I haven't a clue." She tossed two more blue folders on the slippery pile that had built up.

Between the first and second pots of coffee they had rejected the hard kitchen chairs and decamped to the living room, where they now sat cross legged on the plush rug in front of the gas fireplace, which was turned on high enough to provide a warm, dry heat but not so high that they'd be tempted to start pitching files into the flames.

Nick flipped open the next folder on his pile and scanned the pedigree. There were ten members in the family who had agreed to participate in the study, four of whom had been diagnosed with Fenton's Ataxia in their twenties and thirties. The clinical notes were dry and concise, painting a picture of progressive tremors, declining motor coordination, and a life expectancy of no more than fifty years, even with the current drug treatments.

He couldn't imagine why anyone would want to halt the research on such a disease. Find the gene and you might find a better way to treat Fenton's. Find a cure. And then— Nick glanced at the blackened square on the pedigree that denoted an affected male—thirty-five-year-old Frank Knickerbocker might have a snowball's chance in hell to see his daughters—three circles on the pedigree that bore question marks because they were too young to be diagnosed—grow up and have daughters of their own.

Flipping to the clinical coordinator's notes at the back of the folder, Nick grimaced.

Frank Knickerbocker appeared sullen and hostile on the day of examination and did not want blood drawn. Would suggest follow-up consent without wife's presence.

Scowling, Nick added Frank and his family to the smaller pile on the coffee table.

Genie glanced up. "Find something?"

"Not really. Guy whose wife made him volunteer for the study but didn't want to give the blood sample. The clinical coordinator recommended a follow-up."

"Knickerbocker." Genie nodded and grinned at his surprise. "I've got perfect recall, remember? I think there's a second consent form at the end of the file. It turns out he wanted to help, particularly since it looks like he passed Fenton's on to at least one of the daughters. He's just terrified of needles.''

Nick was foolishly relieved to move the Knickerbocker file off the Maybe pile and over to the Not Really pile. There was something about the coordinator's notes that brought the study subjects away from circles and squares on a piece of paper and fleshed them out into living, breathing fathers and mothers and...people.

At Genie's raised eyebrow, he tried to explain. ''This is why I do mostly theoretical stuff. I love the lab. I love the techs and the machines and the way you can ask a complex question, design the experiments to look at your hypothesis, and then never be sure whether you'll have an answer in a day, a week, a month, or even years. That's when luck and synchronicity take over. But this...'' He gestured at the hundreds of file folders and the hundreds more lives they contained in distilled black and white notations.

''They're people.''

He nodded. Of course she understood. She was Genie. ''Yeah. People. Not theories, or test tubes, or little circles and squares on pieces of paper. People. Families. And they're sick. Dying. How can you stand it? Why do you do it?''

''Because they're sick and dying. Because they need me.'' She picked up a lone folder, old and worn from a hundred perusals, and handed it to him. ''Because of Marilynn.''

Nick found the name on the pedigree. Marilynn Churchhill. Born the same year he was, diagnosed with Fenton's Ataxia at eighteen. Her circle on the pedigree was blackened to show affected status. There was a slashing line through it to denote death.

It looked like one of the hundred other Fenton's pedigrees he'd scanned that night except that it was so much older-looking, as if Genie had carried it with her for a long time.

"She was my friend in college, the sister I'd always wanted to have. The mother I never did. She patted me on the head and let me sit with her at dinner and kept the others mainly away when they wanted to pick on the geek."

Nick was getting heartily tired of Genie calling herself that, but before he could say anything, she had rushed on.

"It wasn't until the hand tremors got so bad she couldn't play the piano anymore that I got her to see a doctor."

"It was Fenton's."

Genie nodded and Nick wondered whether she was even aware of the single tear on her cheek. "I graduated that year and went into the research fast track, swearing to her that I was going to find a cure in time to save her. It was foolish. She had an incredibly severe case and was in a wheelchair by the time I took my medical boards." Genie took a deep breath and wiped her cheek with an impatient hand. The wetness glistened orange and yellow with reflected firelight.

"She died a week before I defended my thesis." Genie stared into the fire. "She was my friend."

And for a friend—one of her few friends, Nick surmised—Genie had embarked on a crusade to cure a disease. That explained why she was at Boston General in a linkage lab rather than in some university think tank where they performed higher math with arcane symbols and exclamation points rather than numbers and variables.

Her attacker had picked the cruelest way possible to hurt her. He had not only threatened her person and her lab, he had threatened the very project that was her heart and soul.

Not for the first time, Nick wondered whether the stalker was after Genie personally.

Returning the dog-eared folder to its place, Genie gave a sad shrug and seemed to recall herself from the past. "Well, that was probably more than you ever wanted to know about me, huh?"

Nick shook his head. No, he couldn't say that.

Madness.

"Going to tell me some deep, dark secret now?" she quipped. "Sort of a new collaborator's tit-for-tat?"

Nick had a feeling she wouldn't thank him for telling her his life's story. Besides, he had something else on his mind—madness or not. His fingers itched to touch her and he wasn't sure he could deny himself any longer. Wasn't sure he wanted to. Seeing the love on her face when she'd talked of her friend only made him want her more. He shook his head and leaned toward her. "No, I don't think so. How about we seal the deal another way?"

She didn't mistake his meaning. Her restless hands stilled and he was pretty sure she stopped breathing. She leaned away from him. "Nick. Don't. That is—" She gestured helplessly toward the fire, the house, the files that spilled across the soft rug like a rainbow. "Not a good idea."

She stood, shedding papers as she rose to stand in front of the fire with her fists clenched at her sides. The orange and yellow light glowed through the thin fabric of his favorite shirt, outlining the dusky silhouette of her upper body in warm, pumpkiny tones.

Her arms were slender and the line of her waist shadowed against the light cotton was a sinuous dip and curve that made his palms itch to touch, to savor the feel of the smooth slide across her flat stomach, the hard bump of the nipples that peaked through the fabric as he watched.

He stood and faced her across the sea of colored folders, felt his heart pound in time with the throb of his burned shoulder. "Why not? We're attracted to each other. We're safe here. What could be a better idea than a little welcome-to-the-lab kiss? Or—" He stalked toward her. "Do I have it wrong that you're feeling what I'm feeling?"

"No, not wrong. But look at this place." Genie gestured helplessly at the room around them. "I don't do Cinderella."

"Meaning?" Nick laced his fingers at his back to keep from reaching for her. To hell with not wanting a relationship. He had to have her.

He'd deal with the rest later.

"Meaning that you live in a palace. Have you looked at the rug in the upstairs hall? It's downright scary!"

Want tangled with something darker, uglier. "You don't want me because I have an ugly runner?"

It sounded like something Lucille would've said.

Genie stomped her foot in aggravation and created a mini avalanche of folders. "Don't be stupid, Wellington. It's a beautiful rug. I'm afraid to walk on it, and that's what I'm trying to tell you. You're out of my league. You're the golden boy. The prince. And princes only fall for scullery maids in fairy tales. This is no fairy tale.''

Nick felt his temper—slow to catch on an average week—start to bubble. ''Who said anything about leagues? We're not talking about baseball. We're talking about two mutually consenting adults. You and me.'' He waved a hand at the fire as the hold he kept on the past stretched a little further.

''Well, maybe I'm not consenting, okay? I learned a long time ago not to believe in fairy tales.''

He scowled. ''And you think this is about princes and castles, do you? Well let me tell you a fairy tale then. It's about a brother and a sister and a mother who lived in a castle, but it was no damned fairy tale, because the king was one mean son of a bitch.''

Genie stopped staring into the fire and started looking at him. Finally. Her silence goaded him.

He cursed. ''You want to share secrets? Bare our souls? Fine. But don't complain to me when you don't like what you hear. You think you had it so much tougher because you were smarter than everyone else? Poor little smart kid. Get over it, you were luckier than some. At least your father didn't hit.''

She took a tentative step toward him and he held up a hand to stop her. ''No, you can hear the rest of it. He didn't just hit me—he went after my sister and my mother, too, and when I got in the middle of it he'd just step around me and laugh. He'd tell me I'd have to be better, smarter and faster to beat him—and that I never would be. I never was.''

The memory rolled greasily in Nick's stomach, a familiar cocktail of regret, anger and guilt.

Genie made a small sound of distress. "You were a child."

He cursed again. "I was eighteen when I left. I tried to take my mother and my sister with me, but they wouldn't go."

I love him, Nicky—you don't understand. His mother's words echoed in his head across the years and he fought the urge to hurl his coffee cup into the fireplace. "I couldn't protect them. I thought I could. Then I thought I could take care of Lucille, but nothing I ever did was good enough for her either."

Genie made another move toward him, but Nick held her off with a gesture. The last thing he wanted was her pity.

"Nick, I…"

When she faltered, he smiled grimly. "Not quite the fairy tale you expected, was it, Genius? Sorry to disappoint you. I'm not a prince. I'm just a man and my childhood wasn't perfect, either. But you want to know the difference between the two of us? I didn't let my childhood rule my life."

He crouched down and tossed another log on the fire, not because it needed more fuel, but because he needed to do something with his hands before he wrapped them around Genie. "And you're right. This was a bad idea. Forget I ever suggested it."

He stared into the flames until he heard her leave the room.

Until he was alone.

ACROSS TOWN, THE WATCHER hunkered down between two furry pines and eyed the old Victorian house from the rear. Though several lights had popped on an hour ago, he knew nobody was home. He was just waiting for full dark. Waiting for the silly men in the black-and-white car out front to doze.

He was almost dozing himself when a pair of yellow headlights speared through the darkness and lit the forsythia bush six feet to his left. He cursed and shrank further into the shadows, hoping that the dark knit cap was low enough to cover the bandage that glowed beacon-white.

A car door slammed and a woman emerged. She crossed the lawn and he heard her voice rise sweet and high on the night air as she spoke to the two men in the cruiser.

She was here. He grinned and felt his blood heat in response to her nearness. This was an unexpected bonus—he could retrieve the evidence and have his revenge at the same time. He'd just have to be careful not to disturb the men out front.

He slipped from shadow to shadow, working his way to the back door and freezing when he heard high heels click on the walkway that wrapped around the old house.

"I need to get the spare key," he heard her call toward the front. "I'll just be a minute."

Wonder of wonders. She was coming right toward him. He waited carefully until he saw her reach beneath a painted shingle and retrieve a key. Then he slid out from his hiding spot and grabbed her, clamping his hand over her mouth and his other arm around her body as he slammed her against the wall.

He smiled as she squirmed. They'd danced this

dance before. Then a tendril of her hair swirled up into the glare of the feeble porch light and shone red-gold, not brown. He frowned and spun her around. Saw the sick recognition in her eyes. Cursed viciously.

And hit her.

Again and again.

"THE HELL WITH IT," Nick muttered. He'd been staring at the fire for ten, maybe fifteen minutes. Long enough that his knees creaked when he stood. They popped in complaint when he crossed to the mountainous pile of clinical folders. "It's probably best if we get her back to her real life as soon as possible, right, Q?"

"Mmrph." The white tomcat didn't seem convinced, nor was he pleased when Nick pushed him aside to grab a handful of files.

Q would get over his displeasure. Nick wasn't certain he would, though.

Cassidy, Catzen, Cedars. Apparently he'd taken his handful from the beginning of the alphabet. He flipped through a couple of blue folders, seeing nothing suspicious in any of them. But what were they really looking for? A big yellow star next to one of the names? An arrow with the caption, really Bad Dude, Keep An Eye On This One?

Highly unlikely.

He heard the bathroom door open and shut upstairs and felt like ripping one of the blue folders to shreds, just for fun. She wasn't going to come to him. She never would—particularly after his outburst. Talk about shattering a few illusions and a whole lot of self-restraint at the same time. He couldn't believe he'd slapped at her for resenting her childhood—she had every right. But he'd taken a page out of the Senator's book and aimed right where he knew it would hurt the most.

There were footsteps in the upstairs hall, and rather than be caught gawking up after her like a lovesick mule, Nick glanced down at the blue folder in his hands.

But it wasn't blue.

The Collins folder was gray, with a yellow Post-it on the front that read, "Genie, here're the clinicals on the new family. I got most of it from the Eye Center, though some of the information was lost in a burglary the other day. See the back pages for notes on another phone call I got the other day from the son—Richard Jr. From films FNTN-3 and FNTN-5, it looks like he's an outlier, not a DNA mixup. And have a look at his wife—she seems related somehow, even though she's a married-in. Weird. Steph."

Nick glanced at the first page of the report and figured out that the folder was a different color because it belonged to a different study. The Collins family suffered from Gray's Glaucoma not Fenton's Ataxia.

Wrong disease. He was just about to put the folder in the reject pile when a name caught the corner of his eye. He could've sworn it blinked. That there was a big yellow star and an arrow next to the name—

Fenton.

On an oath, he flipped to the pedigree. The Collins family showed Gray's Glaucoma through four generations, and the second generation had two affected siblings, Mac and Patty Collins, each of whom had large families. The clinical notes on Mac and his family read like a rap sheet.

Mac was in county lockup for sexual assault. His sister Jenna was dead of an overdose, and of Mac's five children, one daughter was in jail for prostitution, one was listed as "unreachable—teenage runaway," two sons had no clinical notes by their names and the oldest daughter was a lawyer.

But it was Mac's younger sister that gave Nick pause. Patty Collins had married a man named Fenton.

Richard Fenton.

The single note beside his name read simply, "Popcorn tycoon." It could have read, "One of the richest men in the northeast."

Nick's fingertips tingled and he fought the urge to curse as he flipped back and started from the beginning of the file. As he read, he became certain of one thing—

They had been looking at the wrong Fenton. It had never been about Fenton's Ataxia. It was about Richard Fenton and his hundreds of millions of dollars. Nick smiled bitterly. If there was one lesson he'd learned well at a tender age, it was that money could make people do some pretty awful things.

He turned back to the Post-it on the front cover. Outlier DNA? He was going to need some help with the lingo. He raised his voice slightly. "Genie? Can you come down here for a minute?"

She spoke from the doorway. "I'm right here, Nick."

"Genie, I need you to explain this note here…"
He looked up. And froze.

She was standing just inside the living room wearing his favorite cotton shirt.

And nothing else.

GENIE HAD THOUGHT she was prepared to take this giant leap. She'd sat on Nick's bed upstairs and given herself a good lecture until her shaking fingers unbuttoned the soft ivory shirt and pulled the sweatpants—his *sister's* sweatpants, she reminded herself—down over her hips so she could kick them free.

She had forced her reluctant feet down the stairs, knowing that even though he said he wanted her, she wasn't sure he still would. His delivery had stung a little, true, as had the knowledge that he thought she was shackled by her past. But could she honestly deny it? Even during her shopping trip with the girls from the lab, she'd begun to wonder how many of her habits were leftovers from the awkward, overbright child she'd once been.

She'd made a mental note to work on it, but hearing it from Nick hadn't been what hurt the most. What had almost torn her apart was the bleakness in his face when he spoke of his father and his ex-wife. Somewhere, somehow, he believed he was at fault for both of them.

Genie could've cried, but she knew him well enough to realize that pity was the worst thing she could give him.

She thought this might be the best, though her knees were practically knocking at the thought of going down the stairs. It might be the best thing for the both of them, but it was now or never—either something happened between them tonight while they were safe behind walls and security systems, or it never would.

Because Genie had a pretty good idea what would happen when all this was over. She would settle back into her stagnant routine in her dull old clothes and the boring new car she'd have to buy with the insurance money from the boring old car that had been blown up. Maybe she'd wear the new clothes Jill and Steph and Molly had forced her to buy, and maybe she'd go out to lunch with them from time to time, but nothing substantial would change.

Nick would slide seamlessly back into his normal life and they'd snarl at each other over sequencer time and argue over the new collaboration—she had no illusions that he wanted to spend time with her, he just knew good science when he saw it. They'd go back to Genius and Beef and every now and again he'd scowl at her and she could imagine that he was picturing her naked.

But inside, she'd be crying. Screaming.

Dying.

Who could have predicted just three days ago that Nick Wellington could become as necessary to her as breathing? It wasn't logical.

Love isn't logical, her brain whispered, and Genie dropped her head into her hands and felt caffeine and nerves hum just beneath the surface of her skin. Her brain was right. It wasn't logical. But the unfamiliar emotion churning through her had to be love. It was too enormous to be anything else.

So it was with equal parts love and fear that she

shuffled through his bathroom and then the bedside table until she found the—thankfully unopened—box of condoms, ripped it open, and slid a couple into the breast pocket of her shirt. She tried not to look at the plastic packets, but her stomach jittered anyway and she had a brief fantasy of hiding in the shower until morning.

Then she had another image of hiding in the shower with Nick until morning, which was enough to propel her across the room and halfway down the hall. Where she stalled. She stared at the carpet. Who was she to dare to love Nicholas Wellington the Third? He didn't even seem to recognize how different they were—tarnished armor or not. He thought he wanted her, but he didn't really know her.

He only knew her as a woman being menaced. As a victim in need of protection. He didn't know *her.*

"And he's not bloody likely to get to know you any better if you stand up here in the hallway all night with no pants on until you turn blue from the cold." Her brave words echoed and she suppressed a shiver. "So get down there and warm yourself up, Genie. Or better yet, get Wellington to do it for you."

Her resolve lasted until she hit the living room door and saw him standing near the fire with a gray folder in his hands and a fierce frown on his face. He called her name without looking up and she answered, stepping into the room, into the light, before remembering that she was nearly naked. "I'm right here, Nick."

"Genie, I need you to explain this note here…" He looked up. He froze. His jaw literally fell open. The gray folder dropped from his fingers and she spared only a second to wonder why he was bothering to look at a Gray's Glaucoma family when she'd been specifically warned against the Fenton's project. Marilynn's project. The one project she would never willingly give up.

His eyes—had she ever really thought them icy?—flashed bright and hot and he took a step toward her, slipping slightly on the piled folders. "Genie?" He stopped at the edge of the couch and jammed his hands into his pockets as though telling himself not to touch her and she resisted the urge to wrap the shirt tightly around her torso and run screaming up the stairs.

Instead she walked toward him until they were an arm's length apart. "Nick?"

He swallowed with an audible click. "What are you doing?"

She had hoped it would be obvious, but apparently it was true what Jill had said, that subtlety was wasted on human beings with Y chromosomes. "I'm pretty sure I'm seducing you. At least that's what I think I'm doing."

"Oh." He swallowed again and seemed rooted to the spot.

Genie blew out a fortifying breath, tugged the sides of the shirt off her shoulders, and let her last item of clothing fall to the floor.

He didn't move, but she could see a pulse pounding at the side of his neck and a light sheen of sweat on his forehead, although that could be due to the fire, which seemed to be pumping out about ten times as much heat as it had been when she'd gone upstairs. He said in a voice rough as sandpaper, "Pity, Genie?"

She shook her head. "Not pity. Not gratitude, either, though I'm grateful for all you've done for me the last few days. None of that."

He moved then, raised his hands and she thought, *Thank God, he's finally going to touch me,* but he simply caressed her face, the corners of her mouth, and said, "Then what, Genie?"

She turned her cheek into his palm and closed her eyes. And lied. "You said it yourself earlier. I want you. You want me. Nothing more."

She thought he whispered, *Thank God,* but she couldn't be certain, and then she didn't care anymore because he was finally touching her, kissing her, and she did the only thing she could.

She kissed him back. With all the love in her heart.

She ran her tongue across the seam of his lips and reveled when he let her in with a moan. He tasted of wine and coffee and rich comfort and sin, and she arched up against him when his hand slid down to her hip then traveled up again to palm her aching, needy breast.

Pressing closer, bowing upward into his hand and his body, she found that the white shirt that had seemed so soft when they sat shoulder to shoulder sorting files was rough against her skin now, sliding deliciously across her chest and belly when he pulled her up against him. The fabric of his pants was slick against her thighs, and he was hard where he pressed against the aching place between them that demanded release.

He tore his mouth away. "Genie, are you sure?"

She knew he was trying to do the right thing, trying not to let her do something she'd regret, but she affected annoyance. "You trying to get out of this already?"

He grinned, a quick flash of white teeth against stubble. "Not on your life." Scooping her up, he tossed her easily onto the couch facing the fireplace and followed her a moment later, pressing her into the soft cushions with the good, heavy weight of his body. He was still completely clothed and she was naked.

It should have been embarrassing.

It was wildly erotic.

He took his mouth on a quick cruise down her throat as her busy hands went to work on his shirt, finding him bare and needy beneath the cloth. His lips slid up the side of her breast and she felt his mouth close over the tip, sending shooting sparks of white-hot light through her body and pulling the pulsing, greedy knot between her legs even tighter. She jolted against him and the breath whistled between her teeth as her fingers dug into his scalp and held on tight.

"Nick! I want… I want…" She was practically sobbing with need and cried out when his fingers found her and danced around the outside of that secret, wet place, soothing and stroking when she wanted them to fill. To inflame.

"I know, Genie. I know. Me, too, but we need something. Protection." He was breathing hard and trying to pull himself away from her even as his hands continued their delicious torture and his slid across hers time and again. "We need…upstairs. Bedroom, maybe. They're up there somewhere."

She loved him for not knowing exactly where they were. She lifted a hand to wave at the doorway at the same time that she draped a leg over his hip, silently urging him to delve deeper. Touch her.

Touch her.

"Over there, I have a few in the pocket of your shirt."

"You brought your own?" His fingers slid a little lower, a little deeper, and she wanted to scream with frustration. Instead she pushed his unbuttoned shirt aside and nipped at his chest hard enough to make him buck against her.

"No. I found yours. They were in the bedside table, by the way."

He laughed in relief and kissed her hard. "You're a genius." And for the first time she liked the sound of that.

She expected that having been given the green light he'd jump up, get the condoms and move things along. But he didn't. He merely smiled and returned to where he had been before—namely teasing at her breasts while his fingers stroked her thighs and her belly, even the backs of her knees, anywhere but where she wanted him to be.

Murmuring a protest, caught somewhere between pleasure and pain, she dragged her fingernails across his nipples and absorbed the quick tremble he tried to hide. He left her breasts and returned to her mouth, but instead of devouring her as she expected— needed—he kissed her soothingly, with aching tenderness that alternately made her want to cry with the beauty and to bang his head against the wall in frustration.

Then, without warning, he ran a finger directly down her center, into her, and pressed his thumb firmly on the coiled knot of desire that was ruling her body.

Genie screamed against his mouth. Her body jerked. And she was flying.

Sensation layered upon layer, coiling tightly and springing free as she was borne along on wings of pure pleasure, on the arms of the man that held her and pressed her up again, higher this time until she shattered into a million, trillion pieces and fell back to earth, still held safely in his arms.

She should have been numb, replete. Boneless. But instead her body hummed with restless energy that surged and pulsed like blood between them. She twined her legs eagerly around his, reveled in the roughness of his pants against the supersensitive skin of her inner thighs while she kissed him and caressed him until he was shaking as hard as she.

Then, finally, he broke free and dove for her discarded shirt and the precious plastic packets in the pocket. When he came back and was standing beside the couch looking down at her, Genie didn't hide her nakedness. She smiled and held her hand out to him. "If you're going to ask me if I'm sure, I might have to deck you."

He grinned and shrugged out of his shirt. "Wouldn't dream of it." His chest was hard and soft at the same time, an intriguing mix of curves and angles that begged her fingers to touch, her mouth to taste. The lower half of his body stood out in sharp relief behind the thin barrier of his tan pants, showing Genie that he hadn't been teasing. He wanted her.

Sliding the soft leather of his belt through the

loops, he tossed the little packet onto Genie's stomach, then joined her on the couch. "Will you do me the pleasure?"

Her fingers shook a little as she slid his zipper down and her heart thundered in her ears. This was really happening. It wasn't a dream. It was happening. It was—

R-r-ring!

They both froze and looked at each other. Nick's face mirrored the dread she felt. "My mother?" he suggested.

Since Genie'd gotten the impression that the two of them weren't close, it seemed unlikely. "How often does she call you here?"

"Never." *R-r-ring!*

"A girlfriend?"

He shook his head. "Nope. Lucille left me with little taste for relationships."

Trying not to let that hurt, she pushed him off her as the phone rang a third time. "Pick it up, then. The not knowing is probably worse than knowing." She wasn't sure that was the truth. As he picked up the receiver and greeted the caller, she hunted up her shirt and buttoned it down the front.

His bare shoulders tensed as he listened, and by the time he said, "We'll be right there," she knew there was something very, very wrong.

"The lab?" She couldn't imagine what there was left to destroy at her lab, except maybe the sequencer and her office.

He shook his head. "No, worse. Steph's hurt." He dragged his shirt back on and grabbed his shoes without looking at her. "We're going to meet Sturgeon at the hospital."

Genie's stomach heaved and she tasted bile. "What happened? Where was she? Was it him? How bad is she?" She couldn't imagine the evil it took to track down one of her employees.

Still avoiding her eyes, Nick grabbed his keys and led the way out of his monstrous house. "She was at your place. She thought she'd help out and feed the cats."

Chapter Twelve

He told her about the gray folder while he sent the Bronco thundering into the night, into the rain.

She held it closed on her lap. "I'll read it when we get there." A pause. "Tell me what happened, Nick."

Closing his eyes against the hot rush of pain and anger wasn't an option when he was running yellow lights at eighty miles an hour, so he kept them open and saw his own guilt in the eerie amber streetlights that whipped past the vehicle. In the white lines that twisted before him, taunting him, because he could never outrun them. Never outrun anything.

"She's just a kid, damn it!" He pounded on the steering wheel and the Bronco shivered in reaction, losing its grip on the wet road and fishtailing through the next bend.

"You're not going to help her by killing both of us. And she isn't a kid, Nick. I'm younger than she is."

"You were never that young." He knew he shouldn't have said that, but he needed to strike out at someone and Genie was handy. "And I'm not going to kill us."

Swearing, he purposefully hit the on-ramp too fast and gained some satisfaction from Genie's gasp and her quick grab at the door handle. Then, with a quick wash of shame, he slowed down, took a deep breath. "I'm sorry. I'm being a jerk right now because I don't know what else to do."

The tense set of her shoulders beneath his favorite shirt told Nick that she'd been hurt by his crack about her age, but she rallied and, with a tenderness borne of...what? She touched his hand where it gripped the steering wheel hard enough to make his knuckles creak.

"What happened, Nick? What did he do? Why?" She poked at the gray folder in her lap. "If what you say is true and we've been looking at the wrong Fenton all along, that still doesn't explain why he'd come to my house. I don't keep much lab stuff at my house."

"I don't know, Genie. I'm not a genius and I can't read his mind." Nick swore again when she winced. "Never mind. I appreciate what you're trying to do, but don't, okay? I just need to fume for a few minutes, until we get to the hospital."

"Fine." She turned back to the window and stared out into the dark rain, her arms crossed beneath her breasts. He had a quick flash of her lying back on his couch, gloriously naked and holding her arms out in invitation. His body thrummed with desire and wanting.

Nick shifted uncomfortably, realizing that frustration was probably responsible for at least half his foul temper. He glanced over at Genie and was rewarded when they passed a particularly well-lit shopping area and the bright neon shone through her shirt and out-lined one breast and a pointed nipple.

He remembered the taste of her flesh, the feel of her flying apart in his arms, and he eased back another notch on the accelerator. Steph had been found quickly by the officers on duty at Genie's house, and she was at Boston General right now under Detective Peters's protection. Genie was right—killing them on the way to the hospital would be counterproductive.

Nick glanced in her direction, but she remained staring out the window, awkwardness etched in the line of her arms and the set of her shoulders. A rush of warm and spiky—not quite lust, not gentle enough to be something else—poured through him, and he sighed, wishing for things he could barely name.

"Sturgeon says it's pretty bad," he began in a thick voice, willing her to turn and look at him. "But she's at BoGen now and they're working on her. She was unconscious when they brought her in."

She didn't turn, but he heard her ask quietly, "She went to feed my cats?"

He nodded though she couldn't see him. "Yeah. She must've figured she'd be safe with the cops out front, watching the place. She went around back to get the spare key and he must've been out there watching. When she didn't come back around the front, Sturgeon's boys figured there was something wrong and went looking for her. They found her by the back door."

Nick remembered Genie's crumpled body stuffed beneath the sink in the developer room and felt the bile rise. It was all too much. They had to stop this creature before he hurt someone else.

"I asked her to feed Oddjob and Galore last month when I went to that conference in Stockholm, so she knew where to find the key. And she was hurt…while we were…" Her voice trembled and Nick took her hand and squeezed.

"Yeah. I know." He felt a measure of sanity return as he threaded his way through Chinatown and pulled into the parking garage beneath Boston General. Enough sanity at least to wonder why the murderer had thought it worthwhile to stake out the house when a pair of uniforms sat out front. "Did you have any lab stuff there that he might have wanted?"

The alternative was that he'd come to finish the job he'd started in the developer room.

She was silent for a moment, thinking. "I've got a filing cabinet full of journal articles in the den, but I can't imagine him having any interest in that. I can't think of anything else, except…" She trailed off and stared down at the pale folder in her lap. "I brought a few films home the other day to review an outlier DNA that keeps not fitting into the proper pattern."

Nick's gut chilled as he remembered the Post-it on the front of the Collins folder. "What family was it?"

She looked from her lap to his face. "The new Gray's Glaucoma family. The Collins-Fenton family."

He shut off the engine with a twist of the key. "Bingo."

They walked side by side through the garage and he was glad for the bustling figures near the Emergency Room door. This was one place in the hospital that never slept. One place where there might be safety in numbers.

Touching her arm as they neared the automatic doors, he said, "Genie. About what happened back at my place—"

She stopped and looked up at him, her bruised face wary, her gray eyes tired and faintly defiant. "Please don't say it was a mistake, Nick. I don't think I could bear that right now. Say the timing was bad and that we'll talk about it after all this is over. Say it was nice and you'll call me, even if it's a lie. But don't say it was a mistake. Don't take it away from me quite yet."

Though he had told himself all those things and more on the ride to the hospital, they had all rung false because the truth was, ill-timed and ill-advised as their interlude might have been, he'd loved every hot, slick moment of it. Every whisper and sigh, every suckle and bite. And given the same circumstances, he'd do it again in a heartbeat.

And again. And again.

So he grinned a fierce grin, touched her cheek while his eyes lingered on her lower lip and he saw the breath catch in the back of her throat, and said, "Sorry, Genius, but you're dead wrong. You might want to recheck your hypothesis the next time you're tempted to put words in my mouth."

"Oh? Then what were you going to say?" She must have tried for an arched tone, but it fell short and came out sounding wistful instead, and Nick felt his heart lurch in his chest.

He lowered his voice a notch, aware that several of the E.R. doctors on a smoke break—didn't they know smoking was bad for their health?—were listening avidly to the conversation. "I was going to say that I enjoyed every minute of it.'' He dropped a quick kiss on her lips, delighted in the way she flushed at the simple contact. ''And that I'm sorry for the interruption.''

Afraid that if they stayed there much longer he was going to drag her off, find a free gurney and an empty exam room to show her just how sorry he was, Nick broke away and headed for the doors.

''Nick?'' He turned back and was fascinated by the quick play of emotions across her face—shyness to temptress, awkward to empowered. She had put her own brown skirt and shoes back on, but kept his shirt. He hoped that was a good sign. She patted the breast pocket. ''Maybe next time.''

He grinned. Nodded. ''Next time. Count on it.''

Then she marched past him, whacking him on the fanny with the gray folder as he passed. ''Good. That's settled. Now let's go get this bastard.''

She strode down the narrow E.R. hallway with her hair flowing freely down her back and an aggressive wiggle beneath the dark brown skirt, and was apparently unaware of the low buzz that followed her.

''Was that Watson?'' Nick heard one masculine voice ask. ''When did she get so hot?''

Nick smiled. She'd always been hot.

She was just a bit behind the curve in realizing it.

GENIE PORED OVER the Collins folder until the little words and the circles and squares of the pedigree began to dance and swirl before her eyes. She glanced at the clock on the green waiting room wall— 2:30 a.m.

''It's Thursday,'' she said to nobody in particular.

She hadn't been to bed since…Tuesday morning. And then she'd been recovering from a concussion, so it almost didn't count.

Nick dozed in one of the hard plastic chairs and she envied him the ability to nap. Detective Peters, who'd insisted on staying with Steph, had poked his head out several times in the past few hours, as had the doctors assigned to her care. They had treated the obvious wounds and had stabilized Genie's new friend, but Steph still hadn't regained consciousness. For all that modern medicine knew about healing the human body, it couldn't always predict the course of a head injury.

She could be in the coma for hours or days. Weeks or months. There was just no way of knowing.

Genie glared down at the gray folder. She was missing something, she had to be. If Nick was correct and Richard Fenton's millions were the motive for the recent attacks, then the culprit had to be someone who stood to lose or gain money based on—what? Whether or not they had glaucoma? That didn't make any sense. The disease was treatable.

"Nick. Hey, Nick, wake up!" He shifted and muttered something foul before his eyes popped open and he half stood.

"What? What's wrong? Is there word on Steph?" He glanced around wildly in search of a doctor or a boogeyman.

"No, I'm sorry. Relax. I didn't mean to startle you, but I need a rich opinion."

He sank back to the chair and stretched, causing all sorts of interesting muscles to press against the white shirt she had unbuttoned five or six hours ago.

Now that she knew what he looked like underneath all that cloth, it was going to be a real challenge to keep her imagination to herself at work. She frowned at the reminder that one of these days—if she lived to see it—she and Wellington would go back to their proper roles.

"A 'rich' opinion as in one that is complex and well-suited to a man of my many talents?"

She shook her head. "No, as in an opinion given by a man with more money than he could ever hope to spend."

Nick scratched his ribs and ran a hand across the fuzz on his chin, which was a darker gold than his hair. "Ouch."

"Shut up and take a look at this." She moved to sit beside him and held out the pedigree. "Which of these players stands to gain or lose the popcorn fortune based on something found in a genetics screen?"

He squinted at the paper and traced the lines of descent with his finger. "Well, Gray's Glaucoma isn't fatal, right?"

"That's correct. Blinding in some cases, but not fatal."

The finger stopped on generation III, Richard Senior's children. "The kids probably stand to inherit the money. Depending on how traditional Richard Sr. is, he might pass the bulk on to this guy—" the finger tapped Richard Fenton Jr. "—because he's the eldest son. Then there are three middle daughters and the younger son."

Genie frowned at the chart. "But they're all pretty normal according to the clinical notes. The scary ones are the descendants of Richard's brother-in-law, Mac.

He's only related to the Fenton fortune by marriage and, according to Steph, Patty and her brother haven't had anything to do with each other since long before Mac was tossed in jail. So how are the sociopathic Collins thinking they'll get their hands on Richard Fenton's money? Assuming we're on the right track, that is.''

Nick tapped the blackened square that represented the eldest Fenton son, Richard Jr. ''Tell me about this guy.''

Recalling from memory, Genie recited, ''Affected with Gray's Glaucoma of an unusually early and severe onset, although his sight was saved by filtration surgery and drops. Seemed comfortable with the study when he was first admitted, but since then, he's called to speak with me about confidentiality issues, just like his father has.'' She paused. ''I haven't gotten back to either of them yet because of all the things that have happened this week in the lab.''

''And his wife? Why is she colored in with pen?''

''Deborah Fenton. I don't know her maiden name. When she came in for the eye exam we require along with blood samples, the ophthalmologist I work with diagnosed her as also having Gray's Glaucoma, which is very strange since she's only related by marriage, not blood.''

''Did Sturgeon ever tell us who's office was broken into over at the Eye Center?''

Genie shook her head. ''Nope, but if you're right about this, I'll bet you money it was the ophthalmologist who saw this family.''

''I never bet on a sure thing, Dr. Watson.'' Nick's

finger traced a line of descent. "What are these diamonds under Richard and Deborah?"

"Spontaneous abortions. Miscarriages. It looks like they're trying to have kids and either their genetic material isn't combining quite right, or she has a reproductive problem that prevents her from carrying to term."

"Dr. Watson? Dr. Wellington?" Peters stood in the doorway, looking uncharacteristically haggard. "Steph— Ms. Andrews is awake. She wants to speak with you both."

But by the time they reached Steph's room, she had sunk back beneath quiet waves of unconsciousness. She looked impossibly young beneath the stark fluorescent lights, and to Genie it seemed unbelievable that the motionless figure lying so still on the hospital bed could be the same woman who'd bragged about her new boyfriend and chivied Genie into buying a dark red dress that didn't suit Dr. Watson at all, but looked just great on the new and improved Genie.

"She's resting comfortably now," said the terrifyingly efficient nurse—the one with the mustache that had so worried Genie earlier in the week.

Dear God, was it really only Thursday?

"Did she say anything while she was conscious? A name or description of her attacker? Anything?"

The nurse pursed her lips, making the fine hairs ripple, and frowned as though trying to decide whether to tell them or not. Finally she nodded and Genie's brain spat out an irrelevant song lyric about being a walrus.

"She said a name. Roger something. But I couldn't

tell if she wanted us to call him, or wanted to tell us that's who hurt her.''

''Roger's her boyfriend,'' Genie clarified, and Sturgeon scowled. She hadn't even noticed his arrival, but he stood near the door. Peters sat by Steph's bed and Genie had a feeling he'd been there all night.

''That's no help.'' Sturgeon pulled an index card and a stubby pencil from his pocket, followed by a shower of empty peppermint wrappers. The translucent plastic bits fluttered to the floor. ''What's his name?''

''I don't know his last name.'' Genie looked to Nick, who also shook his head in the negative. ''But he was the local sales rep for Petrie Pharmaceuticals. That's how they met.''

''That's right, Petrie.'' Nick lowered his voice at the nurse's shushing motion, then gestured that they should all leave. It was obvious that while the doctors were promising a full recovery for Steph, she wasn't going to be in a position to answer any questions for some time. ''Weren't they one of the companies with Fenton's Ataxia patents?'' Then he stopped himself. ''Right. Never mind, wrong Fenton.''

Sturgeon popped a fresh mint into his mouth. ''We're not discounting anything. As soon as Petrie's open in the morning, I'll call about this Roger and see if anything comes up. In the meantime, why don't you two review everything you have on this family and see what you come up with—and what you can use in court.''

Genie felt fatigue drag at her. She'd forgotten about that little sticking point. ''Like what? Someone has to see him attack me?''

"That'd do it, though I'd rather not go that far." Sturgeon looked at her gravely. "It would help if you remembered what happened to you in that darkroom. Maybe you saw his face."

She took a deep breath and glanced sideways at Nick. "I'll go in there again. This time I'll turn on the dark lights. Maybe that will trigger something."

Red lights splashed like blood against the warm, cloying darkness. The smell of chemicals, excited man, and—what else?

She shook her head in frustration. She had to make her brain behave. Had to.

"No way. I won't let you do it. That's ridiculous, Genie. Don't you remember what happened the last time you went in there?"

"I remember," she replied, and let her face show him just what she remembered. She remembered kissing him. Needing him.

Wanting him.

"I'll station uniforms on the lab floor. You'll be safe," Sturgeon promised, but Nick only snarled.

"I won't let you do it."

Tired beyond words, Genie couldn't take it anymore. She had to get some sleep before she screamed. "Let it go, Wellington. We'll talk about it tomorrow." She glanced at the wall clock, which now showed that it was four in the morning. It would be dawn soon. "I mean later today. I've got to get some sleep someplace safe."

"I'll drive you to my place," Nick offered, though he was swaying on his feet.

"You're too tired to stand up, never mind drive. Detective, you said there were uniforms on the thirteenth floor already?'' Sturgeon nodded. ''Then I'm going to my office. I don't know about you, Wellington, but I've got a folding cot in the closet for those experiments I just can't leave alone overnight.''

Nick nodded. ''I've got a really comfy chair that does me just fine. I'll walk with you.''

SHE BRUSHED HER TEETH in the eerily empty bathroom and heard the water gurgle down the pipes as she thought of how soothing she used to find sleeping alone in the lab.

Not anymore.

But she consoled herself with the fact that she wasn't alone now. There were two police officers in the elevator lobby, and Nick…well, Nick was around somewhere. He'd disappeared right after they arrived on the floor and she hadn't seen him since.

The cot unfolded to a narrow six feet, plenty of room for her though not enough to share. Not that Nick seemed inclined to stay with her. The single pillow and pair of blankets might have seemed primitive in other circumstances, but after a head injury and nearly fifty hours without sleep, Genie would have dozed on cement and been grateful for the few minutes of peace.

But once her head hit the pillow and her eyes closed, she found she couldn't sleep. The events of the past few days, both wonderful and horrible, churned and spun in her brain until she couldn't tell where one ended and the next began.

There was a noise in the darkened doorway and Genie tensed, knowing that she must be safe, but scared nonetheless. She cracked an eyelid and relaxed. It was Nick.

Not really wanting to talk or to argue or to even be awake all the way, Genie lay still. He watched her for a moment as though memorizing her, and then he turned and dragged a cushioned chair into the doorway. He sat, tilted it back so he could rest his head on the door frame, put his feet on the opposite wall of the narrow office corridor, and was snoring softly in minutes.

And, not long after, so was Genie.

NICK AWOKE WITH AN enormous crick in his neck and an annoying squeaking sound nagging at his ears. He shifted, groaned, and nearly fell off his desk chair as it tilted and spun at the same time, a stuffed and wheeled bronco trying to dump its rider in under eight seconds. The squeaking paused.

"You're awake."

It wasn't the most enthusiastic of greetings, but Nick supposed that "good morning" was a little inappropriate under the circumstances. Besides, with a day's growth of beard on his chin, the imprint of textured wallpaper on his temple, and something really revolting growing on his teeth, he supposed that "awake" was about all he could claim.

"Yeah. Seems so." The squeaking resumed as Genie bent her head over the lightbox on her desk and rubbed at a film with a wad of tissue. A squeeze bottle of pure ethanol—rubbing alcohol—sat at her elbow, and as he watched, she directed a thin stream at the film and rubbed off another set of pen marks. "Make a mistake?"

She muttered something and he half expected her to tell him that geniuses didn't make mistakes, but instead she pushed away from the desk and stood, pressing her hands to the small of her back and arching. She was wearing a flowing navy skirt now, with a white shirt that had a touch of lace at the wrist and neck—she obviously kept a change of clothing at the lab for emergencies just as Nick did—but she hadn't bothered with a bra. As she stretched, Nick saw the darkness of a nipple slide past the fabric, and he wished he could walk across the room and press his lips to that place. Wished he could wet the cotton over her breast with the tip of his tongue and tease the flesh beneath to a rosy point.

Wished he could lock the office door, clear the scattered films off Genie's desk and finish what they'd begun the night before. He ran a tongue around his mouth and amended, *After I go find that toothbrush I left in the break room.*

Genie frowned and sat back down, shaking him from his imaginings of them in the office, the break room, the gel room.

The darkroom.

She shook her head and poked at the films. "No mistake, this just doesn't add up."

Nick slid his chair into the office so he could read the films across the desk without breathing on her. He saw that the films, crisscrossed with pen lines and radiograph shadows, were labeled with the names of the Collins/Fenton family. "What're you trying to do?"

"I'm trying to haplotype this family."

Nick knew a haplotype was a way to look at longer

stretches of DNA to figure out relatedness. A child should inherit one haplotype from each of his parents. Brothers and sisters should share, on average, half of their haplotypes. Cousins should share one fourth, and so on.

Something niggled at the back of Nick's brain as he bent over the films. "You can't figure them out?"

Genie shrugged. "I can figure them out, but they don't make sense. See Richard Jr.?" She pointed to a blackened square. "He's got both of his mother's haplotypes, which should only happen if his parents are closely related, which they're not. Then look at his wife, Deborah." Genie pointed at a darkened circle. "Not only does she have the disease—which she shouldn't, because she's a married-in—but she's got haplotypes that make her look like she's related to this bunch." She pointed to the Collins branch, with their jailbirds and runaway daughters. "I'm beginning to think this family's DNA got royally mixed up during the blood draw and that we're on the wrong track entirely."

She sighed, rolled her head on her neck. "Maybe we should be thinking more about those drug companies. I wonder whether Sturgeon's found Roger from Petrie yet. I called the hospital already and they said Steph's resting comfortably, but is still unconscious. Peters is still with her."

Nick glanced at the clock and was surprised to see that it was early afternoon. But he supposed it made sense since they hadn't gone to bed—well, in his case gone to chair—until nearly dawn. He wondered how long Genie'd been up. She looked tired.

And beautiful.

He cleared his throat past a sudden tightness and asked, "Can she have visitors?"

Genie nodded. "I asked Molly to take one of the officers to my condo and pick up these films before she went to see Steph." She lifted the sheet of translucent gray plastic to the light and frowned over a mark. "Does this band look like this one, or this one?" She pointed on the film to three black bars that looked identical to Nick.

"Um. You're the expert. Why don't you keep working on this while I call my friend at the patent office to ask about Petrie." And have a little chat with Richard Fenton Sr., although he wouldn't tell Genie about it. The call would probably be a breach of both her ethics and Nick's responsibilities as a collaborator, but frankly he didn't give a damn.

He had a gut feeling about the Fenton family, and it was telling him there was something not quite right in the popcorn empire.

Chapter Thirteen

When Genie was finally done with her analysis, she pushed away from her desk and stared.

She got it now. She knew what was going on.

Her finger traced the single line she'd inked between Richard Jr. and his true father—his uncle Mac Collins. Then the double bar between Richard Jr. and his wife Deborah—who had been called Dolores Collins before she ran away from home.

Where a single horizontal line on a pedigree meant "married," a double line indicated "consanguineous marriage." Marriage between blood relatives.

Then Genie touched the sad little diamonds beneath Richard Jr. and Deborah. No wonder Deborah had Gray's Glaucoma. No wonder they couldn't have children.

They were half brother and sister.

And no wonder Richard Sr. was leaning on her for the DNA results. He must suspect something and not want the shame of demanding paternity tests.

Genie breathed deeply. She understood now. And ethically, she couldn't use any of it.

She knew Nick would probably stomp around and

holler when he found out, but there was no way she could take what she knew to Sturgeon. What she'd just discovered was bound by confidentiality as surely as she was bound by the oaths she had taken to become a doctor and a genetic researcher.

There had to be another way. There had to be some piece of information she could use to nudge the detectives in the right direction. Something they could take to court that didn't rely on the blood samples and DNA information she had sworn to keep confidential.

There had to be a way she could save her own life. And Nick's. Because as surely as blood ran through her veins, the monster that had been born of an unholy union would be coming for her—motivated by shame and greed and a wife who shouldn't have been.

Think, Genie. Think!

She was left with conscious information she couldn't use, and unconscious information she couldn't get at. If only her brain would behave enough to let her into that deep, dark pocket in the very back where it had stored her memories of those minutes in the darkroom. If only.

She closed her eyes and strained, tried hard to force her way past that black curtain, and got only the same flash of black-red and heat and noise.

And saw…nothing. It was no use. She couldn't do it out here in the light and the sun. She would have to go back into the darkroom. All the way back.

A tight band of nerves settled across her chest and Genie felt a greasy, uncomfortable churn in her stomach and a bead of sweat on her forehead. She thought she might be sick.

"No. You can do this," she told herself, and shivered with a sudden chill. Catching sight of a flash of ivory hanging on the back of her chair, she grabbed the shirt she'd borrowed from Nick the night before and pulled it on over her sensible navy clothes.

Suddenly she was warm again. More than warm, she was heated, and a shimmering coil strung through her as Nick's scent rose up to enfold her, giving her strength. She hugged the shirt tight and heard a crinkle from the breast pocket. Touching the little packet like a talisman, Genie smiled, took a deep breath.

And walked back into the red-black darkness of memory.

NICK HUNG UP the phone with a feeling of satisfied dread in the pit of his stomach. There was no Roger at Petrie Pharmaceuticals, and Richard Fenton Sr. had admitted that the strange son whose paternity he'd come to doubt sometimes went by the nickname Roger.

Sturgeon was on his way to pick up Richard Jr. Everything was going to be okay.

His stomach rumbled greedily and Nick looked at his watch, the Rolex that Genie had once derided as a fake. It was midafternoon and he wasn't sure what meal he was hungry for, but he figured it was time for Genie to take a break regardless. He headed for her office, waving at the two uniforms in the elevator lobby as he passed.

They could call and have some spring rolls and Pad Thai delivered by the place around the corner. A few waters from the machine down the hall, a little light from a portable alcohol burner and, voilá! Instant picnic.

And after, for dessert... Something growled within Nick, a different kind of hunger.

A voice echoed in his head. *Don't crap where you eat, boy.* Nick shook his head. "Stuff a sock in it, Senator."

He burst into her office, full of good news and energy and the knowledge that the bad stuff would soon be over. And the good stuff just beginning. "Genie?"

She wasn't there.

Dread clutched, sudden and complete as it tore at his heart and closed his throat. "Genie?" Louder now, but his hail wasn't answered. Not from the lab. Not from the hallway. Not from the break room. And not even when he stuck his head into the ladies' room.

He was almost to the elevator lobby, ready to knock the officers' heads together for letting her leave the floor without protection, when he heard a familiar clanking groan, an exhalation of pent-up air forced through ducts by a churning, newly repaired behemoth.

The X-ray developer.

Nick took a step down the hall, which suddenly seemed a mile long. An enormous shiver crawled down his spine.

Forcing his feet to move, he tapped on the revolving door. "Genie, it's me. Are you okay in there?"

There was no answer, but with an ominous *rubba-thump, rubba-thump,* the door spun so the opening faced Nick, inviting him into the blackness of the light lock, into the uncertainty of the room beyond.

As he stepped into the lock, Nick wished fleetingly

for the pipe wrench, for a metal film cassette, for anything heavy and weapon-like. *Rubba-thump, rubba-thump.* The darkroom was warm and filled with the sound of the developer, the smell of chemicals and the eerie whine of red lights.

Digital numerals hung suspended in the red-blackness, flickering between a hundred-twenty and a hundred-fifty volts as a forgotten gel box sent killing current through a buffer-filled chamber. Standing just inside the narrow room, Nick was almost blinded by the almost total absence of white light.

"Genie?"

He sensed rather than saw movement in the corner by the industrial sink and fumbled at his back for the switch.

"Leave the light off, please." Her voice was calm, though he thought he felt her hand tremble when she touched his arm. "I need your help."

He nodded in the darkness and, as his eyes adjusted, he began to pick out the lighter color of her shirt against the dull cabinets, the glint of her eyes and teeth against the black circle of her face. "Of course. Anything. But I wanted to tell you what I've learned about Richard Fenton Jr.—"

She cut him off with a finger on his lips. "Later. Right now I need you to help me remember. I'm so close I can even see the place in my mind where the memory should be. But I can't reach it. Can't find it." Nick heard a rustle of cloth as she moved across the room, saw her shadowy figure turn to face him.

"How can I help?" But he had a pretty good idea what she was asking, and he wasn't proud of the twin spirals of lust and revulsion that moved through him at the thought of playing the rapist's part.

"Stand over there, by the chemical tanks. I'm going to turn the dark lights off and leave, then come back in and turn them on again."

"They'll take forever to come back on once you've doused them. Why not just leave them on?"

"Because I'm pretty sure that's what happened that day. It was pitch-black in here, which is why I didn't notice him until it was too late."

"Okay. Are you sure this is necessary?" Nick stepped back into the farthest reaches of the room, away from the light. Away from sanity.

"I am. I need to know, Nick. And this is the only way. Okay?" Whether she saw him nod or just assumed from his silence that he'd play along, she continued. "Wait until I'm all the way in the room, then grab me from behind and push me up against the sink."

The idea repelled him.

The idea excited him.

He balked. "If you can remember so much, then why do you need to do this? Why not—" She stopped him by flicking out the lights and plunging them both into complete, terrifying darkness broken only by those flashing numerals. One hundred-twenty volts. One hundred-fifty.

"Just do it, please? I need this."

She left the room through the revolving door, leaving Nick alone with the darkness and the chemical smell and the pumping, throbbing sound of the X-ray developer.

He pressed his back against the solid strength of the cement wall and put himself inside the mind of a monster.

GENIE GLANCED AT THE elevator lobby and reassured herself that the officers were still there. Then she ran a hand down her borrowed shirt and stared into the gaping maw of the light lock. Her stomach fluttered and her chest tightened. *There's a man in there,* she told herself, *and he's going to grab you and touch you and make you remember exactly what happened.*

But it wasn't just *a* man in there, ready to snatch her from behind and push her up against the sink with his body. It was Nick.

Nick was going to grab her. Touch her. Breathe in her ear like a lover.

She lifted the collar of his shirt to her nose and sniffed, trying to bring to mind the warmth and safety she'd found in his arms before. But caught in the twilight between memory and reality, she smelled only developer chemicals and blood.

Rubba-thump, rubba-thump. The door was loud as a death knell, the room darker than a moonless night. Genie was alone as she stepped out of the rotating door and flipped the switch down, heard the whine of red lights struggling to warm up when they'd barely begun to cool.

Then there was a hand across her mouth, choking off the scream that leaked between her teeth, and a hard body pushing her from behind. She stumbled the few steps it took to cross the room and banged into the sink, felt a starburst of pain as her hipbone glanced off the stainless-steel rim. She whimpered and the pressure let up for a moment, then returned even harder as her attacker pressed his muscled stomach against her lower back to hold her in place.

"What now?" His voice was thick and unsteady, and suddenly Genie wasn't in the pitch-black with a faceless murderer. She was in the warm, intimate confines of the darkroom with Nick.

He loosened his hold on her jaw to let her answer. "You put your other arm around my torso. No, higher than that." His arm slid upward until it rested just below her unbound breasts. His thumb lay along her rib cage, and if he moved it just a bit, he would touch her nipple—and know that it was hard as a pebble.

"Like this?"

"Yes." It was barely a breath, and she thought she felt him tremble, a fine shiver that raced through them both. "Now, push me against the sink with your, um, pelvis. Not your stomach. Lower."

"Genie, I'm sorry. I can't, I'm…"

She knew what he was trying not to say. That he was holding his lower body away from her on purpose, that he was as aroused as she and likewise ashamed. "It's okay. I understand, Nick. Just do it, please?"

And he did, curling around her with a low groan as the hard bulge below his waist fit precisely in the cleft between her buttocks. He surged against her once, pressing her stomach against the metal sink as he slid up and down, rubbing his length against her backside a single time as though unable to stop himself.

Genie whimpered at the heat that flowed through her as the black-red room took a long, lazy spin and her insides melted, reminding her that she'd left her panties in Nick's bathroom the night before and hadn't had an extra pair in the office. She was bare beneath the loose navy skirt, and the thought of him separated from her by only a few layers of cloth was almost enough to send her over the edge. She felt a single trickle of wetness slide down her inner thigh and pressed her legs together to catch the sensation.

Nick was breathing hard now, and those fine tremors raced from him to her and back again as his breath fanned her cheek and his hand slid away from her mouth to cup her jaw as though it was an anchor.

"And now?" His voice whispered against her ear, hot and insistent, and she whimpered again.

And remembered.

Through the gory light she could see the silhouette of a man, the glint of teeth and tongue. Chuckling at her feeble struggles, he licked the side of her neck from shoulder to ear.

"Now you lick my neck."

She thought she heard him curse but he complied. But he didn't just swipe his tongue from her ear to her shoulder as the other had done. Nick took his time, bending his head to her collarbone and nibbling his way up while his hips pistoned in a mindless, insistent rhythm that was as old as evolution. When he reached the soft spot beneath her ear, he lingered, puffing quick breaths against her lobe before he took it in his mouth to suckle.

The sensation tore through her and Genie almost jackknifed in his arms, crying out as the curtain shredded and the little room in the back of her brain was suddenly lit with bloody-red light.

We're smarter than you think, Doctor. We figured

*out what you and the old man are up to. And we're
going to stop you. Permanently.*

"Genie? Genie? Are you okay? What happened?"
She held his arms fast when he would have pulled
away, shook her head when he would have demanded
answers.

She remembered. She remembered everything. And
she didn't care anymore.

She cared only about the feel of the man that held
her, about the shape of his maleness pressing against
her from behind, insistent in its desire, and the smell
that washed over her as she breathed hard in the aftermath of memory.

Developer chemicals and Nick. That was all.

And it was everything.

Without a word she held his forearm across her
throat, leaned into its support as she guided his other
hand down and helped him pull up the loose navy
skirt and find her, bare and waiting. She angled away
from the sink to give him room and reveled in his
strangled moan.

"Dear God. Please tell me he didn't do this." But
even as he spoke, Nick's fingers slid deep into her as
his erection pressed against her from behind, then released as he withdrew his fingers. Pressed. Released.
In. Out.

Genie shuddered in reaction, feeling the pressure
build, feeling the helix tighten. "No." She was almost sobbing now, straining against the gentle im-
placability of his forearm across her collarbone. "No.
This isn't about him. This is about us. Only us."

Reaching awkwardly between them behind her
back, she cupped him through the soft slacks and was

rewarded by a strangled oath and a sharp, unexpected movement of the fingers within her. She felt the tidal wave build, willed it back.

Went to work on his zipper, freed him to lie heavily against her buttocks. To pulse hotly through the thin navy cloth that separated them.

"Us?" His chest heaved when she pressed back into him, wiggled a little to torment. "Just us?"

He freed both hands to lift the back of her skirt, and he slid himself beneath her, under her from behind so that his ready flesh curled around her center and touched that greedy, dewy nub that wept for him.

"Us. You, Nick. I want to make love with you." She nearly sobbed when his hands slid under her shirt to close on her aching breasts, and he set a maddening rhythm from behind, sliding his pulsing hardness back and forth across the outer lips that shielded the place that yearned for him to fill it.

She thought he muttered an oath, but the words were muffled against the side of her throat as he laved her with his tongue, caressed her turgid breasts, and pumped her from behind.

Genie moaned wordlessly. It was too much.

It was not enough.

She twisted in his arms and grabbed at his hair to hold his head in place while she poured into him with a kiss, tried to tell him with her body that she wanted him. Needed him.

Loved him.

With a growl he boosted her up so she was sitting on the waist-high counter, at the corner between the sink and the long bench. He spread her legs wide, folded the navy skirt up to her waist and looked. Simply looked in the red darkness.

Genie couldn't bother to be embarrassed. She was too hot, too needy. So instead of covering herself and shying away, she bared herself to his gaze and found no shame in the gesture. She felt beautiful.

The red lights glistened off the moisture that pearled at the juncture of her legs and off the wetness on her inner thighs. It gleamed on the length of his shaft, where it had rubbed against her liquid center. And it splintered off Nick's Rolex watch when he reached into the breast pocket of her borrowed shirt with a teasing finger and withdrew one of the condoms she'd taken from his bedside table not even a full day before.

He sheathed himself, protecting them both, and she braced herself for the moment she'd only experienced once before, with— No. She wouldn't think of him now. Wouldn't ruin this moment with thoughts of a past that wasn't worth remembering. Wasn't important anymore.

But when she thought the moment had finally come, Nick surprised her by returning to her mouth, kissing her deeply with a rhythmical thrusting of his tongue that set off similar pulses deep within her. Needing to be closer to him, to feel the steady strength of his body, she slid forward on the counter and wrapped her legs around his waist while she tried to unbutton his shirt to feel the thump of his heart beneath.

When she found it, it wasn't thumping. It was galloping. Racing. Threatening to burst out of him. Her own blood burned in response, charring Archer's memory and blowing it away on a hurricane of greed. She ripped at the rest of his buttons, sending them flying, and tugged at the pants that still hung at his hips, urging him to move faster. To hurry. *Hurry!*

But there would be no hurry. Nick worked his way down across one collarbone, then fastened his lips on a nipple, suckling it through the cloth of her lacy white shirt. Genie moaned and let her head fall back while her legs clutched at him, begging. He paused to torment the other breast as one hand wandered to her bare thigh, played for a moment making paths with the wetness he found there. And then he pressed his thumb square on that tight little bud and she bucked.

And screamed his name.

The developer groaned in response, its noise drowning out almost everything else, and the red light seemed both darker and brighter all at once. Then Nick replaced his thumb with his mouth and nothing seemed like anything at all, because Genie was lost in a sightless, soundless whirling vortex of sensation that ripped through her like a tornado and stayed there, swirling and churning and pulsing until she didn't think she could take any more.

And then Nick stood, pressed his forehead to hers and plunged into her in one fierce, slick motion, and Genie discovered that there was more to feel.

So much more.

The heat roared through them both and swirled around the red-black room, catching the scents of developer chemicals and hot, rampant lovemaking. Genie opened herself to Nick and felt him inside her, felt him touch her heart. Her soul. And felt the need and the tension begin to build again. Only this time it was stronger, more consuming, clawing at her with velvet talons and demanding that she take Nick deeper. Harder. Faster.

On a roar, he pulled her off the counter and held her against it so her hips were pinned between the film cabinet and his body. So he could thrust deeper. Fill her more fully. Make love with her until the tears came to her eyes and the pulsing began deep within her, in a place she hadn't even known existed, and grew in ever-widening spirals to include him as she clenched his hard flesh in a dewy vise and he gripped her hips with bruising fingers and drove into her, through her one last time and his body bucked and shuddered.

And her name tumbled from his lips like a prayer.

THE DEVELOPER GRUMBLED its customary song and the red-black lights made Genie's hand, tangled with Nick's, look like a rose in the twilight.

She felt him sag against her, slide out of her, and she put her feet to the floor with a pang of regret. She wished they'd made love the night before, in front of the fire where there would have been an opportunity for soft words and cuddling. There was neither time nor place for that now. Not here, where there were two uniformed guards in the lobby and a nightmare of recessive genes hunting her.

Nick didn't speak, leaving her to break the loud silence in the clanking developer room. His chest heaved and he braced his palms against the counter, let his head hang as he sucked air into his lungs.

She didn't have to be a genius to figure out that in

the aftermath, he felt awkward about the situation. Disappointment shimmered softly at the thought that he was more interested in the chase than the cooldown. But he'd never claimed any differently. He'd made it plain he wasn't looking for anything meaningful. His father and ex-wife had seen to that.

Genie would've cursed them, but she hadn't the energy.

"Well, then," she said, smoothing the navy skirt down over her legs and lingering over the unfamiliar trembling in her thighs. If she never had another moment alone with Nick—and the thought was almost too painful to bear—then at least she'd have the memory. And everyone knew her memory was her best feature. "I'm going to stay in here a few more minutes and make sure I've remembered everything important. Can you go call Sturgeon?"

Nick finally moved. With a shudder, he pulled himself upright and fumbled in the red darkness. Genie heard the sound of his zipper, the splat of the condom hitting the waste basket in the corner, and made a note to remove it before the cleaning staff came to empty the garbage.

"Sturgeon? Remembering? Is that all that was to you, a freaking mnemonic?" Disgust laced Nick's tone and Genie stepped back, stung.

"Of...of course not. But you were— I thought..." She blew out a frustrated breath. This was another one of those things they didn't teach in grad school—making conversation after spontaneously combusting, memory restoring, multiply orgasmic sex.

Lovemaking, insisted her brain.

"Never mind." Nick swore. "I'll go call Sturgeon

and meet you in the break room in ten minutes.'' And with an angry *rubba-thump*, he was gone. The darkroom was empty.

So very empty.

Genie slumped back against the stainless-steel sink and pressed her hands to her aching eyelids. She didn't need the time alone to remember. She and Nick knew what had happened and why, and even had information she could ethically give Sturgeon. All of the facts were neatly lined up, one following the other like a well-designed experiment.

The only piece of the week's puzzle that refused to be put into a space was Nick.

Where would they go from here? Soon she and Wellington would be free to return to life as usual. He could keep his silly Face of Erectile Dysfunction poster on his door—though she now knew firsthand that it was a lie—and go on with his Rolex-wearing, mansion-living existence without feeling as if he was leaving her unprotected.

And she could wear her stupid old-person clothes and drive her boring new car and work until ten every night and grow old in her little condo with a pair of cats named after characters in a fictional spy series.

Then she heard movement out in the hall. *Rubba-thump, rubba-thump.* The light lock cycled and she wasn't alone anymore.

''Nick?'' Maybe he'd come back to fight. Maybe he'd come back to take her in his arms, kiss her, and vow his undying love. Yeah, and maybe she had been popular in college.

Then the red lights clicked off and the fluorescent white lights came on, momentarily blinding Genie.

She pressed back against the sink as the man, a blurry silhouette against the harsh glare, came toward her.

It wasn't Nick.

Her eyes finally cleared and she blinked him into focus. He was slightly under six feet tall, dark-haired and handsome in a rich, pampered sort of way. His hair was artfully done, his nails manicured and his expression haunted.

It seemed odd to meet the owner of the DNA she'd pored over all morning and to realize that, except for a few red-black images, he was a stranger.

Nick. Where are you? I need you. I need help!

She stalled, trying for cool when she really wanted to scream. A trickle of sweat ran down the side of his face and his hand trembled, index finger tightening convulsively on the trigger of the neat black pistol in his hand.

"Richard Fenton Jr., I presume? Or should I call you Collins, like your daddy?"

He giggled, a high-pitched, unnerving sound against the rumbling backdrop of the churning film developer.

"You figured it out. Dolores said you'd figure it out and that's why we had to stop you. Old Fenton's been looking for an excuse to cut me out of the will for years, and once you told him I wasn't his kid, it'd be goodbye to all that lovely money. And if you told anyone about Dolores being Deborah and Deborah being Dolores, then they wouldn't let us be together anymore. She said so."

"What are you going to do?" Genie couldn't keep the quiver out of her voice.

He raised the pistol, aimed it at the line of stitches on her eyebrow, and giggled again.

"Elementary, my dear Watson. I'm going to kill you."

Chapter Fourteen

"Excuse me? Dr. Wellington?"

Nick looked up in surprise. The young, dark-haired woman at the break room door shouldn't have been there.

"How did you get in here? Are you with Peters and Sturgeon?" He'd left messages at Sturgeon's desk, on his cell phone, and his beeper, so it was possible he'd sent a co-worker over to the lab.

She shook her head, came all the way into the room and closed the door. Nick stood slowly.

"I'm going to have to ask you to leave. This floor is closed to visitors and staff because of some recent trouble Dr. Watson and I have been having."

"Don't worry, I have an I.D." She smiled and flashed a passkey bearing a picture of a pretty red-head. Stephanie. "I know all about your troubles, and I'm sorry for the inconvenience. My brother Richard should have just killed her in the first place and been done with it. Instead, like husbands always do, he messed it up, and now I'm going to have to clean things up for him. Again."

Sick certainty chilled in Nick's gut. This was the

piece Richard Sr. had known nothing about. The wife. From the look in her eye, the woman was mad. Cold. Wouldn't even hesitate to take care of Nick before she finished off Genie.

If Nick let her. This time he would be smarter. Faster. Better. He had to be, or Genie was dead. He held out his hands and stepped toward Richard Jr.'s wife. "I'm certain we can work something—"

"Stop moving right now, or you're going to be sporting a few new cavities." Nick hadn't seen the gun until it appeared in her hand, pointed at his chest. It looked like a police-issue weapon.

She followed his gaze. "Nice, isn't it? I borrowed it from one of the gentlemen in the lobby. It's amazing how many men are surprised when a woman overpowers them. Sexist, don't you think?"

Nick managed a strangled, "Um," and wondered desperately how much longer it would be before Genie joined him for their meeting in the break room.

He'd planned to apologize for his complete lack of coherence in the aftermath. There had been so many things he'd wanted to say, but she'd beaten him to the punch and her complete nonchalance over the whole incident had just plain irritated him. So much for candlelight and soft words—even if his own desire for them had been a shock.

But now he hoped she wouldn't come for him. Hoped she'd stay in the darkroom for a long time, at least until Sturgeon apprehended Richard Jr. and got his message.

Assuming Sturgeon had found the man.

"Don't worry about your girlfriend," the woman suggested with a smile. "Richard's taking care of her right now." She licked her lips. "And this time he's not going to mess it up."

Nick swore as a parade of images flickered through his mind. Genie in the elevator with her soft gray skirt and her high lace blouse. Genie crumpled under the darkroom sink with blood on her lab coat and a man's fingerprints on her throat.

Genie laughing at something he said, sighing over a shared Bond moment, humming in pleasure as though grilled cheese and tomato soup was haute cuisine.

Genie crumpled under the darkroom sink with blood on her lab coat. Not moving.

With a primal roar, Nick launched himself at the woman, who smiled as if she had expected the move. Coolly, she pulled the trigger as he flew toward her, and in Nick's mind the image would be forever engraved of the look on her face the moment the police officer's gun jammed in her hand.

Then as she cleared the jam and fired a wild shot, he hit her in a full-body tackle he had perfected during the weekly, somewhat unorthodox Biochemistry Department basketball games. She went down, hard.

And didn't move.

FINGERS PRESSED TIGHTLY against the lip of the developer room sink as though the cool metal could somehow help, Genie tried again to calm the shaking, sweating man with the gun.

"I wouldn't have told anyone about the DNA results, Richard, you have to believe that. Do you remember signing papers the day you had your eye exam and gave blood?"

Richard Fenton Jr. shook his head doubtfully. "Not really. I remember that my father—no, Richard Sr.— told us the whole family was volunteering for research, like we were lab rats or something. It sounded like fun at first, but once the nurse explained everything, Deborah got real mad. She wanted to leave and not give blood, but Richard Sr. said we had to and she doesn't like to sass him. She says if we're nice to him, we'll inherit the money we deserve when he dies."

His simple speech pattern and occasional tic made Genie think that either he'd never been particularly smart or recent events had put him right over the edge. When you were dealing with first-degree relatives making babies, anything was possible.

"Well, we have your signature on the piece of paper that says we can't tell anyone else about what we find in your blood. It's yours, and we can only use it for research. Even if your father had called and asked me about the results, I wouldn't have told him." Genie didn't mention the fact that Richard Sr. had done just that.

"Daddy and Dolores said you'd tell him if he promised you enough money. That's how he does things. With money. Our money—Deb's and mine." Richard Jr. rocked back and forth on his heels, humming slightly, and Genie's heart nearly broke for the man. Whatever connection he'd had to the world at large had been severed by the events of the last five days.

She didn't know how Richard's mother had come to be pregnant with her brother's child, but with Mac's jail record it probably hadn't been pretty. And it seemed that the twisted old man was still controlling things from maximum security.

"Richard, how did you meet your wife?"

He snickered, scratched his ear with the muzzle of the gun, and resumed pointing it at Genie while the developer churned loudly in the small room and the odor of chemicals boiled around them.

"She ran away when we were both kids, but her father found her. He told her about me when he was dying of liver cancer in county lockup. Only he didn't die. He's too powerful to die. He sent her to help me. Sent her to make sure I got the money I deserve."

Crack! The sound was muffled by the thick block walls and the pounding beat of the film developer, but Genie thought it had been a gunshot. Nick. Nick was out there with Richard's wife and she was armed. Or was it one of the police officers finally doing his job?

She had to get out of the developer room. Nick might need her. He might be hurt.

That he might already be dead was a possibility she refused to consider. She slid a step to her right, talking to keep Richard focused on her voice, not her position.

"Did you know he was your father?"

Richard shook his head and, out of the corner of her eye, Genie saw the voltage flash from one hundred-twenty to one hundred-fifty and back again as the vertical electrophoresis unit sent killing current surging through the open buffer chamber. "Not then. She told me on our wedding night."

Feet pounded in the hall.

Richard Jr. shifted uneasily and Genie talked loudly

over the noise of the developer to cover the sounds from outside, just in case it was Nick or the officers coming to her rescue.

If it was Dolores/Deborah, she was already doomed.

"That must have been quite a surprise, finding out that you'd married your half sister." Even as the words left her mouth, Genie wished them back. Richard's face clouded and he took a menacing step toward her, gun held at the ready.

"Don't say it that way! It wasn't wrong! She loves me and I love her and it's our money, we deserve it! It wasn't wrong."

"Okay, okay. I'm sorry." Genie slid another step to the right, now keeping the high counter at her back. She repressed a shiver at the quick memory of Nick's heavy body pinning her against that same counter as he pumped himself inside of her, lifted her higher, sent her spinning. Nick. Her heart thumped at the memory, then died a little at the thought that Nick could be in the outer lab, hurt. Needing her.

She slid another step to the right and kicked something metallic that pinged a protest and skittered across the floor.

"What? What was that?" Richard glared at her. "What are you doing? Where do you think you're going? Stop right there." He bumped up against her with his body and shoved the gun beneath her chin. Genie stood almost on her tiptoes, trying to relieve the sudden pressure, the immediate threat. "You hurt me the other day—I'm gonna get you back for hurting me, and so is Deborah. She doesn't like it when people hurt me."

"I didn't mean to hurt you, Richard." She tried to keep her voice calm, but it quivered anyway.

Think! She had to think her way out of this one. Her captor's eyes were getting wilder by the second, his body was warm and hard where it pressed against hers, and she could see a line of stitches behind his right ear where she'd hit him.

She saw movement out of the corner of her eye, and at first thought it was just those digital numbers blinking their mindless current change. But then it happened again, a slow, measured slide of the revolving door, and Genie realized that the light lock now faced outward to receive a new person.

Nick! It had to be Nick. Richard's wife wouldn't bother with stealth. She'd just come in with a loud *rubba-thump*. It had to be Nick.

And Richard would shoot him.

"Not so smart now, are you, Doctor?" Richard jabbed the gun a little higher into the soft flesh beneath Genie's jaw and she whimpered. Satisfaction glinted in his eyes and he poked the gun again at the same time that he ground his hips against hers. She tried to squirm away and he grunted. "Like that, do you? Well then, why don't we—"

Rubba-Thump! Rubba-Thump! "Drop it, Fenton!"

Richard swore sharply and spun them so Genie was in front of him, a human shield against the furious man who now stood in the tiny room. "Don't do anything foolish, Wellington. You wouldn't want your little girlfriend to get hurt, would you?"

Nick. Nick was here, he was okay, Dolores hadn't hurt him. The words chanted a mindless litany through Genie's brain and she smiled at him as though she hadn't seen him for weeks. Then Richard shifted the gun to her temple and the smile died.

One-twenty. One-fifty. The numbers fluttered again and both Nick and Genie glanced over at the vertical electrophoresis unit. Their eyes met. A silent message passed.

"If you let Richard and me walk out of here together, he won't hurt me. He promised." Genie licked her lips and tried to bring some moisture to her fear-dried mouth.

"I did?" The pressure from the muzzle at her temple eased up, then returned. "Oh, yeah, I did." He pushed her toward the light lock. "You let us out, Wellington, and nobody gets hurt." He paused. "Where's Deborah? What did you do to her?"

"I— Nothing. She's waiting for you outside." Nick swallowed and Genie learned something new about Nick Wellington.

He was a terrible liar.

Unfortunately, Richard noticed it, as well. "You lie! What happened to her? What did you do to her? I'll kill you!" He turned the gun away from Genie's temple to point it at Nick. "I'll kill you!"

And it seemed that everything happened at once. Genie kicked backward, digging her heel into Richard's shin just as Nick leaped at the other man and grabbed his gun hand. A shot went wild and the sound of shattering glass echoed above the churning of the developer and the swearing of the men.

They tussled briefly, and when Richard fired again in Nick's direction, Genie grabbed a film cassette and thumped the smaller man behind the ear, right where the stitches were, and fresh blood bloomed.

Richard howled and straightened, clapping his free hand to his head and staggering toward the counter. Genie hooked his ankle with her foot and pulled, and Nick pushed the yelling man's shoulder on the way down, aiming him directly at the vertical electrophoresis unit.

He fell on the counter with his chest across the warm glass plates and his gun hand in the buffer chamber. Richard stiffened, his eyes rolled back, and as Genie screamed and threw herself against Nick's broad chest and felt his arms come up to hold her, Richard began to jerk uncontrollably as the current arced across the metal of the gun and into his body.

One-seventy. Two-twenty. Three hundred.

The digital numbers climbed and Genie buried her face in Nick's shirt, unwilling to watch a man die but unable to make herself walk away. When the numbers passed four hundred, the safety fuse in the charger blew and the unit quit.

Richard slid to the floor and lay still. Then his chest jerked once. Twice. And he began to breathe.

Genie and Nick stared down at him for a long moment, then at each other. "Are you okay?" They spoke simultaneously, then laughed a little at the absurdity of the question.

"Did he hurt you?"

Genie shook her head. "Not really. He was more confused than anything, I think."

Nick tightened his arms, wincing at the warm, wet feel of the shirt on his back. The shrapnel wound must've broken open again. "I've never been so scared in all my life as I when I realized you were in here with him and I couldn't get to you. I—I'm sorry I took so long.''

Thumping him lightly on the chest, Genie scowled. ''Will you please get over feeling like you've always got to do one better? You saved my life. Not once, but at least twice this week—do you see me complaining?'' Her voice softened. ''Thank you.''

The truth of it shimmered through Nick like warmth. He hadn't been too late. He'd protected Genie, and she hadn't complained—not once. She wasn't Lucille.

And he wasn't his father.

He was his own man, a man in love with Genie Watson. And this time it would be okay. He held out a hand to her.

''About what happened…before.''

Genie shied away from the hand and hugged herself as though she felt a sudden chill. ''We don't have to talk about that right now, do we? I mean, you've been up front from the beginning that you don't want to be involved—''

''Genie, I love you.''

''And I knew all along that…what?''

He grinned at the expression on her face, at the sudden lightness in his chest. ''I love you. I want to marry you. Make babies with you. I want to listen to you sing in the shower and I want to read the snippy little memos you'll send me about picking up my socks, and I just plain want to *be* with you for the next lifetime or so.'' He reached for her. ''What do you say?''

She backed away and almost tripped over Richard Jr.'s unconscious form. ''But you're… But I'm…''

She blew out a frustrated breath, then paused and glared at him. "Are you trying to save me again, Wellington? Because if you are…"

He shook his head and spread his arms wide. "I'm nobody's prince or savior. I'm just a lonely man in a big, empty castle, and you're the woman that I love. I'm not trying to save you, Genie. I'm asking you to save me. Will you marry me?"

He saw the decision in eyes that flooded with tears, and he felt his heart explode in his chest as she finally, finally, nodded and hurled herself at him. Kissed him. Said, "I love you, too. Oh God, yes, I'll marry you."

And as they kissed long and sweet, Nick heard the commotion outside that heralded the arrival of Sturgeon and his men—too late to see the mystery end.

But just in time to see a new love begin.

Epilogue

"Oh, darling, you look so lovely." Vivien's accent made the words lush and wonderful, and when she gently adjusted the coronet of flowers that held Genie's veil in place, Genie touched her hand.

"I'm so grateful you helped me plan all this, Mother. Everything looks perfect."

"Oh, pooh." Vivien waved the compliment away as though flying to the U.S. on a day's notice and arranging a fantasy wedding in two weeks was nothing. But Genie saw the sheen of tears in her mother's eyes and knew the time together had meant as much to Vivien as it had to her.

She couldn't have her childhood back—and wasn't sure she'd change it if she could—but she could take control of the future.

Her and Nick's future.

Peeking between the heavy draperies at the bright light of a perfect, sunny Florida day, Genie scanned the assembled crowd. Nick had remembered the "dream vacation" she'd once shared with him, and had flown them—and their friends—to Disney for a big, tacky wedding. It was perfect.

She waved at her brother Etienne and he grinned and waved back, giving her a big thumbs up. Steph sat next to him, wan and bruised, with her daughter Jilly in her lap. Only time would heal the young mother's wounds, thought Genie. Time and friends. She saw Detectives Sturgeon and Peters sitting behind Steph, saw the younger man watching Steph as intently as he had while she lay in the hospital—and wondered.

Her gaze touched on Nick's sister, who smiled in response. Nick's parents had been ''too busy'' to attend, but the members of both labs were there in force, along with a cartoon mouse who should have looked out of place, but didn't. Standing beside the mouse was a big blonde. The sight of him made Genie's heart swirl giddily in her chest and she gazed up at Cinderella's castle towering majestically in the background.

''I always wanted to visit a place like this,'' Genie whispered. ''Do you think it's too silly for Dr. Eugenie Watson?''

Her mother took her arm in a shy hug. ''Maybe, but I think it's just right for Genie Wellington.'' The music swelled from hidden speakers and they saw a few curious faces speckling the edges of the cordoned off area, waiting to see the bride. ''Now, let's go get your prince.''

Genie barely felt the measured steps that brought her down the aisle to Nick's side. She barely heard the minister's words, hardly noticed the giant cartoon character standing off to one side. She could only feel.

She felt the warmth of the man beside her. The pressure as he slid a gold band woven in the shape of a DNA double helix onto her finger. The touch of his lips on hers.

And all the awe and wonder and love that anyone—even a genius—could possibly feel as he took her hand and they walked toward their friends.

Together.

*   *   *   *   *

Watch for Steph's story,
SECRET WITNESS,
from Harlequin Intrigue in March 2004!

HARLEQUIN®
INTRIGUE®

has a new lineup of books to keep you on
the edge of your seat throughout the winter.
So be on the alert for...

BACHELORS AT LARGE

Bold and brash—these men have sworn to serve
and protect as officers of the law...and only the
most special women can "catch" these good guys!

UNDER HIS PROTECTION
BY AMY J. FETZER
(October 2003)

UNMARKED MAN
BY DARLENE SCALERA
(November 2003)

BOYS IN BLUE
A special 3-in-1 volume with
REBECCA YORK (Ruth Glick writing as Rebecca York),
ANN VOSS PETERSON AND PATRICIA ROSEMOOR
(December 2003)

CONCEALED WEAPON
BY SUSAN PETERSON
(January 2004)

GUARDIAN OF HER HEART
BY LINDA O. JOHNSTON
(February 2004)

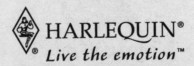

HARLEQUIN®
Live the emotion™

**Visit us at www.eHarlequin.com
and www.tryintrigue.com**

HIBBONTS

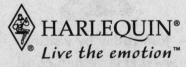

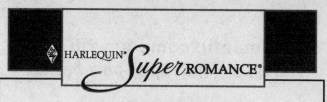

It's romantic comedy with a kick
(in a pair of strappy pink heels)!

Introducing

HARLEQUIN®
flipside™

"It's chick-lit with the romance and happily-ever-after ending that Harlequin is known for."
—*USA TODAY* bestselling author Millie Criswell, author of *Staying Single*, October 2003

"Even though our heroine may take a few false steps while finding her way, she does it with wit and humor."
—Dorien Kelly, author of *Do-Over*, November 2003

Launching October 2003.
Make sure you pick one up!

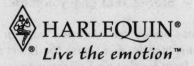

HARLEQUIN®
Live the emotion™

Visit us at www.harlequinflipside.com